Wheel of Death

A Mystery by 22 Authors

from

Cozy Cat Press

This book is fiction. All characters, events, and organizations portrayed in this novel are the product of the author's imagination or are used fictitiously. Any resemblance to actual persons—living or dead—is entirely coincidental.

For information, email **Cozy Cat Press**, cozycatpress@aol.com or visit our website at: www.cozycatpress.com

ISBN: 978-1-946063-63-2

Printed in the United States of America

1 2 3 4 5 6 7 8 9 10

To all the Cozy Cat Press readers

Chapter 1
by Bart J. Gilbertson

Glory Lockhart took one last look at herself in the car's rearview mirror. She didn't understand why she felt so nervous. It wasn't like she'd never been on a date before. Then again, the last time she *did* go out on a date was almost thirty-five years ago. Glory reached up, and with the palms of her hands, softly pushed up her lightly graying hair, first on this side, and then on that. With arched eyebrows, she quietly critiqued her appearance and then with a soft moan and a roll of her eyes, she reached up again and pulled her hair behind her ears into a ponytail and secured it with a small band. Much better. It was simple yet effective. She didn't want to look like she was trying too hard. She just wanted to have some fun. Glory turned and opened the car door. *Here I go.*

She slowly walked across the gravel between the silent cars in the parking lot, hearing the familiar crunch under her feet. Sounds of the carnival began to grow louder with each advancing step, and she pulled her shawl around her a bit tighter when she felt a gust of the cool night air. She took in the swirling, colorful lights and the smells of roasted cinnamon nuts, popcorn, and other delights reserved for fair days. She smiled to herself. This wasn't going to be so bad. Then she felt another pang of nervousness.

Maybe she was nervous because she was meeting a man she'd never met before in her life. Maybe she was nervous because he had chosen to meet her at the county fair in full view of everyone else. In a small town of only 2,100 people, everyone she knew was sure to be there. She could just hear Gladys Prior now, telling everyone in Rainbow's End about it. Did you see the *man* that Glory was with last Saturday night? *Quite the scandal*! Glory knew that her best friend, Connie, would come to her defense. It was Connie who'd convinced her to go out on this blind date in the first place.

Her date was an old friend of Connie's husband. *If Connie said he's all right, then he must be all right*, Glory told herself. Maybe she was nervous because she was approaching fifty-five years of age. The last time she'd had a date was with Ron, her husband of thirty-one years, before he passed away a year ago. Maybe she was nervous because she was the mother of four and the grandmother of three. She could imagine the look on her date's face when she told him that. Then again, she really couldn't imagine it, after all, because she didn't even know what his face looked like.

Maybe she was nervous because of all of the above. *Yeah, that's it*, she decided. It was everything put together.

Before she knew it, she was at the entrance. A large, arcing sign above her read, *Welcome to Rainbow's End*, and then in smaller letters underneath was another sign that read, *May you find your treasure at the end of our rainbow*! Glory smiled. *That's new*, she thought to herself. She wondered who came up with that cute little slogan.

Glory lowered her eyes to take in the sights. Whirling rides with bright lights and blaring music were scattered all around her. Booths of various sizes and heights were interspersed between the rides. Tables and benches were tucked away here and there. People of all ages were milling about carrying all sorts of things—cones of cotton candy, oversized stuffed animals, and the occasional water-filled bag with a lone goldfish jiggling about inside. It was a beautiful, Vermont summer evening. Everyone was smiling and having a great time. In fact, Glory realized with a wave of relief, she didn't even recognize anybody. Maybe she had no reason to be nervous after all.

"Tickets, lady?" The apathetic voice came from a small ticket booth just to her left. Glory turned to see a young girl with jet black hair inside, sitting on a high wooden stool. She blew a bubble with her gum until it popped and then quickly gathered it back into her mouth with her tongue. The girl leaned forward, elbow on the counter, and placed her chin on an open palm. Still chewing her gum, she said again, "Do you need to buy some tickets?"

"Oh, no, not yet. I'm meeting somebody," Glory said. "By the way, where is the Ferris wheel? That's where my friend is waiting for me."

The girl lifted her other hand and pointed to her left, without looking away. "In the center of the park. Can't miss it."

"Thank you." Glory offered the young girl a warm smile. The girl managed a weak one in return.

As Glory made her way down the concourse, she noticed some of the attractions. There was a house of mirrors, a haunted house ride, a handful of kids' rides with small airplanes and rocket ships that went up and down as the ride went around in circles, a petting zoo, a freak show, food booths with the usual corn on the cob, foot-long hotdogs and, of course, cotton candy. There were booths that tested your skills as a ping-pong ball tosser, a Skee-Ball roller, and as a marksman. As she made her way to the center of the fairgrounds, she found all of the larger rides. Some of them gave her motion sickness just from looking at them. And then, there it was. Right in front of her. The Ferris wheel.

She stopped in her tracks to look around it first. She was hoping to spot him before he saw her. There was a line of people, some of whom were young couples holding hands, waiting for their turn on the ride. To the right was a man sitting on a bench, leaning forward with his head between his knees. Apparently, he'd gone on one ride too many. That couldn't be him, could it? A young woman stood a few feet behind him yelling at someone on her cell phone. It was hard to tell if she and the man on the bench were together or not. Glory continued looking around. There was another man dressed as a clown carrying a bunch of helium-filled balloons, walking slowly around the base of the ride. Definitely not him. To the left, leaning against a pole, was another man, cupping a lighter in his hand to fire up a cigarette. Too young.

Then she saw him. An older man, standing by the fence in front of the ride with his hands shoved deep into his pockets, also seemingly looking around. She wasn't sure how she knew it, but it was him. This was her date.

Almost immediately after she'd spotted him, he turned and stopped when he saw her. She saw the flash of a smile as he took a step forward. He pulled his hands from his pockets and walked her way.

"Oh, shoot," she said, under her breath. She couldn't remember his name! She desperately tried to remember what it was. She gritted her teeth and readied herself as he closed the distance between them.

He stopped before her and extended his hand. He had a friendly face and warm eyes. He was dressed comfortably in denim jeans and a plaid shirt. Very clean and presentable. He had a full head of dark hair, flecked and graying on the sides. Kind of rugged, but not overly so. He was a nice-looking man. Glory smiled up at him.

"Glory?"

"Yes."

"Hi, I'm Tom. Tom Rankin."

She let out a small breath of relief. He'd bailed her out of that one. She accepted his hand and shook it. "Glory Lockhart."

"It's so nice to finally meet you," Tom said, withdrawing his hand. "I'm relieved to see that you seem to be normal. You never know what can happen with these things, you know?"

Glory smiled at his well-meaning comment. "I try not to shock anyone."

Tom softly laughed. "Good. Your first name is very unusual. Is that your given name?"

"Yes. My mother had a penchant for the out-of-the-ordinary."

"Well, I think it's a lovely name."

"Thank you, Tom. You … uh, yours … too," she said, with an immediate cringe.

Tom placed his hands back into his front pockets and gently rocked on his heels. "So, what would you like to do first? There's no shortage of things to do around here."

Glory looked around tentatively. "Anything is fine, just as long as it isn't too crazy. I'm not as young as I used to be."

Tom smiled. "Don't worry. I'm on the same page." He looked around and then pointed to a booth behind her. "How about that shooting gallery? I'll try to win you one of those stuffed animals over there."

"Sure. Works for me."

As they walked over, they could hear the booth operator shouting, "Step right up! Five shots for five dollars! Win a prize! Don't pass this up, now. Five shots for five dollars! Step on up here and take your best shot and win a prize!"

"What can I win?" Tom said, pulling out a five dollar bill.

"If you hit one out of five duckies, you get five tickets. Five tickets will get you on one of the smaller rides. Two out of five duckies, and you can have your choice of ten tickets, or one of these smaller toys here. Three out of five duckies will get you twenty tickets or a large toy or stuffed animal. Five dollars will give you five shots. Come on and win a prize for the missus!"

"What if I hit four out of five? Or all five?"

The operator stopped and smirked. He shook his head and said, "Nobody hits four or more."

"But, what if I do? Then what can I win?"

"Tell you what," the operator leaned in, "if you hit duckies with all five of your shots, you can have your pick out of all the prizes I have hanging here."

Tom nodded. "Okay."

A few minutes later, they walked away from the shooting gallery. All three of them. Tom, Glory, and the life-sized, golden brown teddy bear with the bright red bow tie that the attendant had handed her.

"Wow," Glory said. "I'm impressed. Where did you learn to shoot like that?"

"Desert Storm."

"Well, I've never seen shooting like that ever, and I've been around guns pretty much my whole life."

Tom looked at her curiously. "You've been around guns?"

"Say," Glory said, shifting her newly won prize to her other arm. "Do you think you could carry this for me? It's almost as big as I am and it's getting kind of heavy."

"Oh, sure!" Tom took the bear from her and tucked it under his right arm like it was no heavier than a jacket. "Sorry about that. So how is it that you've been around guns?"

"Well, before he died, my husband was the chief of police here in Rainbow's End for the last twenty years or so. Our oldest son, Tyler, is also on the force. He'll more than likely become the chief himself someday."

"Wait a minute," Tom said. He stopped and looked at her. "You were married to Chief Lockhart?"

"Yup. Ron Lockhart. For thirty-one years. We had four children together. All boys. Tyler, Cameron, Chance, and Joey. All good kids. They look out for their momma," Glory said. Her face showed a hint of pride. "Sometimes, I feel like Barbara Stanwyck's character from the Western television show, *The Big Valley*. Only she had three sons, and I have four. I guess you could say we're a modern-day version of the Barkleys." Glory softly laughed at the notion. Telling him about her kids wasn't as hard as she thought it would be.

"So, you're *that* Lockhart," Tom said.

Glory looked over at him in mild surprise. "Is that a bad thing?"

Tom didn't respond at first, as if he hadn't heard her. Then he quickly turned to look at her and smiled. "No, no! I didn't mean to imply that. It's just that it didn't register with me who you were when Connie told me about you. It just clicked into place. Makes sense now."

"So, you knew my husband?"

Tom shook his head. "No. Not personally. I knew *of* him. How did he die?"

"He was killed in the line of duty. A routine stop gone bad."

"Oh." Tom looked down. "I'm so sorry. I hadn't heard. Did they catch the guy?"

"No. They never did. He got away."

Tom looked back over to her. "You'll have to forgive me. I honestly didn't mean to put such a damper on our first date. I apologize."

Glory smiled and patted his arm. "Don't worry about it. It happened well over a year ago. We've learned to accept it and move on. I'm doing okay."

She could see the relief in his eyes. "I'm glad to hear that," Tom said. He looked around them. "What should we do now?"

Glory sidled up next to him and took his arm. "How about you take us on the Ferris wheel?"

"Us?"

"Yeah, us. Me and my teddy bear."

Tom laughed out loud. "Okay, let's go."

As they walked over, Glory looked up at him. "Speaking of registering something, I just registered the fact that you said it was our first date. Does that mean there are going to be more?"

"If you'd like there to be."

"Yes, I think so. I'm having a good time."

"Me too," Tom said. "What is it that you do, Glory? Do you also work for the police force?"

They walked up and got in line. The clown was still there, as well as the man on the bench. Only now, the man on the bench was lying on his side, apparently still recuperating. The younger man who had lit a cigarette was gone. Standing at the same pole, however, was a different man. He was simply leaning against it, looking around.

"No. I run a small antique shop on Main Street. It's called Glory Days. Between the shop and my boys helping me out every once in a while, I make do. Sounds pretty boring, huh? An antique store on Main Street?"

"I don't think so. I think it fits you just fine."

"What?" Glory said, moving slightly away. "You think I'm an antique?"

"What? No! No, not at all! That's not what I meant," Tom stuttered, surprised.

Glory tilted her head back and laughed. "I'm just kidding with you, Tom."

Tom smiled. "Ahhhh. She has a sense of humor, too."

The Ferris wheel stopped and the operator motioned for them to get on.

"Looks like it's our turn," Tom said.

They stepped up to the ramp and while the operator held the seat steady, they climbed aboard—Tom first, taking the seat on the far left, then Glory, sitting to the right, and the teddy bear wedged between them. The operator latched the small gate shut, made sure their seat belts were clipped in, and then pressed a button to move the wheel up a notch, allowing the next people in line on.

"I have to admit it's been years since I've been on a Ferris wheel," Glory said.

"Me too, actually."

Soon, the wheel began to move around in its customary circle. Glory gripped the side bar for that added feeling of safety. She looked over at Tom who seemed to be having a good time. But then, as they circled back down toward the ground, she noticed Tom glance sideways at the crowd of people. A sudden look of fear crossed his face and he began to visibly shake.

"Tom? Are you okay? What's the matter?"

"Uh, yeah. I'm fine. I'm okay, Glory."

"What is it? Talk to me."

Tom looked over at Glory, nervously biting his lower lip. "Glory ... I have to admit something, too." The words sputtered out of his mouth, almost incoherently.

Glory furrowed her eyebrows. "What?"

"Oh, god." Tom laid his head all the way back and looked up at the sky. He slowly began to shake it from side to side. "I didn't realize the hole I'd dug for myself until just now."

Glory turned to face him completely as they once more reached the apex of the wheel cycle. To say she felt alarmed would have been an understatement.

She pressed the teddy bear out of the way. "Tom, what's going on?"

He closed his eyes. "I *did* know your husband, Glory." Tom abruptly sat up and looked at her with imploring eyes. "But, it's not what you think. Believe me, it's not." Desperation lined his voice. "I knew Chief Lockhart."

They came down and swung past the starting point once more. Tom leaned his head back and closed his eyes again, then slumped against the bear that was situated between them. He didn't say another word.

"Tom? Tom?"

Glory looked over the side of their carriage seat and thought she saw someone running through the crowd in the opposite direction, then the wheel hit the topmost point and began its descent yet again, and she lost her line of sight. Since they were the first to be let on, the Ferris wheel stopped at their cart first to let them off.

The operator lifted the gate and Glory unlatched her seatbelt and got off the ride. "You have a lot of explaining to do, Tom Rankin!" With a playful scowl on her face, she turned around.

However, Tom remained where he was on the ride, still slumped against the bear.

"Tom?" Glory called out. This wasn't funny anymore. "Tom! Get off the ride."

"I'll get him, miss," the operator said. He moved over to Tom and shook him by the shoulder.

Unresponsive, Tom slid down behind the bear and lay there, unmoving. "Dang, lady. What'd you give him to drink anyway? He's gassed," the operator called back, in a half laugh. Some of those waiting in line laughed also.

"Nothing. We didn't have anything to drink." Glory took a hesitant step closer.

The smile on the operator's face faded and he turned back to Tom. He leaned over to try and coax him awake, then stood up and jumped backwards."Oh lord!"

"What's wrong?"

The operator turned to look at Glory, his face ashen and drained.

"Your friend ... he's dead!"

Chapter 2
by Rae Sanders & Annie Irvin

The next half hour was a blur for Glory. Someone from the first-aid station had covered Tom's body with a blanket. He lay on the ground with his head turned toward the hot dog stand, eyes closed as though he could be asleep. The blood soaking through the rough gray fibers of the blanket told a different story, however. Glory thought the blanket looked scratchy. Then she remembered Tom couldn't feel the roughness of the material and tears started to fall. She hadn't known him very long, just over an hour, but he was a human being, and it bothered her that his life had ended so quickly.

The first cops to arrive on the scene were her son, Tyler, and his partner, Alice Henson. In his police uniform, his stride purposeful, his shoulders squared, Tyler was a young version of his father.

As chief of police, Ron had always been able to keep his cool and throw on a poker face when he needed to. Glory watched Tyler's expression change from inscrutable to one of total surprise as he spotted her standing next to Tom's body. Well, he wasn't the chief yet.

"Mom, what in heaven's name are you doing here?" He pointed to the body. "Is this someone you know?"

Before Glory could answer, the medical examiner arrived to do his job. Dr. Bob Johnston was a few years older than Glory and had been at this for over forty years. At a crime scene he was respectful of the dead and also good with the living. Glory had known Bob for years and he gave her a much needed hug now.

"Sorry you had to see this," he said, patting her hand before he turned away to take charge of the body.

"Mom," Tyler said, his tone a mix of concern and disbelief, "let's go sit."

Glory knew that when Tyler had started his watch this evening the last thing he would have excepted was to find his mother at a crime scene. He and Alice led her toward the cruiser parked on the street that ran along the edge of the fairgrounds. Glory had been married to a cop for enough years to know the two were going to question her about what happened. She wiped her eyes on the tissue Alice handed her and tried to be as concise as she could.

"We had only been here about an hour," she told them.

"Was this your first date with him?" Alice asked.

"What?" Tyler's voice rose an octave. "You were on a date?"

"Yes, dear," Glory said, shooting a quick glance at Alice. "It was a blind date."

"A blind date?" Tyler's voice was almost in the dog-whistle range now.

Glory ran a hand over her hair. *Her gray hair*, she reminded herself as she glared at Tyler. She was more than old enough to date and didn't need her son's permission.

"Yes, Tyler, I was on a blind date. His name is Tom Rankin. We were having a nice time until the Ferris wheel started on the final go-around. Then Tom quit talking." Glory shivered. "That must be when it happened. After we stopped, I got off but Tom didn't move. The Ferris wheel operator tried to roust him and that's when he noticed the blood on Tom's back and a hole in the seat's backrest. What happened next is kind of foggy to me."

While Alice radioed dispatch to run a check on the deceased, Tyler asked a few more questions and made notes.

"Did you hear any shots fired?"

"No, but the Ferris wheel is in the middle of the rides and they all blast music. There was a huge crowd of people milling around and it was noisy. Besides, we weren't that far from the shooting gallery."

"Did you notice anyone hanging around Tom or following you two this evening that made you feel uneasy?"

"No, not really."

"Not really?"

"Well, toward the end of the ride, Tom acted like he saw someone in the crowd below that he knew. He really seemed afraid. I asked him what was wrong but he didn't give me a straight answer. He did say he knew your father."

Tyler raised his eyebrows inquiringly. "He knew Dad?"

"Yes, so he said. 'That Lockhart' was how he put it." Glory rubbed her temples. She felt a headache coming on. Her first date in over thirty years and look how it had ended. Tom Rankin was dead.

"So was he a friend of Dad's? I mean, you never met this fellow but went on a blind date with him, is that correct?" Tyler's voice had a scolding tone to it.

"It was a *blind date*. That entails I'd never met him. And I take it you're asking me that as my son, not as someone on the force."

"Maybe I'm asking as both. You never know where questions will lead you—if you get honest answers, that is. You'll have to bear with me. It's a little shocking when you find out your mother is dating by being called to the scene of a shooting."

Glory scolded back. "I suppose it is. Maybe I should

have broken you in more gently and picked someone out of a police lineup to date."

"It's late," Tyler said, slipping his notebook into his pocket. "We'll take you home. The chief might have you come to the station tomorrow and add to your statement."

Putting aside all thoughts of how a man could be sitting next to her talking one minute and dead the next, Glory said, "I drove my own car here."

"At least there's that," Tyler mumbled under his breath.

Glory gave her oldest son a pointed look. "I would like to get my bear."

Tyler paused, looking at her. "Okay, I give. What bear?"

Glory pointed to the now shutdown Ferris wheel where several police officers were questioning people while others tried to clear the area and keep a crowd from forming. The only passenger left on the Ferris wheel was the big stuffed teddy bear.

"Tom won it for me earlier," she said simply.

"Teddy looks like he's part of a crime scene now, Mom. We'll have to leave him."

Alice smiled kindly at Glory. She and Tyler had gone to the academy together and had been partners since their first day on the force. She gave Glory a covert wink. "I'll make sure to get Teddy to you when he's no longer a suspect," she said.

"I'll drive you to your car," Tyler told his mother.

Glory knew her son was upset with her and frankly, she didn't need that tonight. He would just have to deal with whatever was gnawing at him. Ron had been gone for a year, and it wasn't as if she had run out the first weekend after his passing to hang out at a bar and pick up men. *That* would really have set the gossip mills grinding in Rainbow's End. Of course, tonight's tragedy would be fuel enough to keep that fire going for quite some time.

A few minutes later, Glory slid behind the wheel of her car and buckled up. She needed to get to Connie's before word of Tom's death reached there. Tom and Connie's husband, Max, had been friends and Glory didn't want either of them to hear of this through the grapevine. Besides, she had some serious questions to ask her friend.

Glory pulled into Connie's driveway and glanced at her watch. She was surprised to find that it wasn't all that late. So much had happened in such a short amount of time. She sat gathering her thoughts for a minute before she opened the car door and stepped out onto the concrete. A chorus of crickets and katydids filled the summery night air along with the sweet scent of heliotrope and 4-o'clocks. Glory felt herself relax a bit.

Connie and Max lived in one of the older homes in Rainbow's End. They had found the place right after they married and both had fallen in love with the hundred-year-old home. Max was just out of the service and working for his father. The elder Mr. Robertson was a general contractor, so Max and Connie had been able to lovingly restore every square inch of their home. Max had insisted they keep as much of the original as possible, saying the old wood captured the character of the house.

If Max's stamp of expertise showed on the exterior, Connie had outdone herself on the interior, often with antiques she'd found in Glory's shop. She loved old things almost as much as Glory did. The two women had a lot in common, from antiques to gardening to experimenting with new recipes in the kitchen. They were close—which was why Glory had agreed to go on the blind date with Tom in the first place.

Tom. How was she going to tell them he was dead?

Before she reached the front steps, Connie and Max were standing in the doorway waiting for her. It was clear by the look on each face that they had already heard the news.

"How did you hear so fast?" Glory asked as they gathered around the white oak kitchen table. Max got himself a beer and offered her one. She shook her head. She wouldn't mind a beer right now, but wanted to keep her head as clear as possible—at least until after she asked Connie and Max all of her questions. After that, she might take him up on his offer.

"Rainbow's End gossip," Connie said, tucking a wavy lock of bobbed brown hair behind her ear.

Glory should've known.

"First off, five different people called to tell me they had seen you with a strange man at the fair," Connie added.

Max took a swig of his beer and scratched at his graying mustache. "We even heard about the giant bear you were toting around."

"Nothing like attention to details," Glory said.

"I've heard three different versions of this already tonight and I'm sure by tomorrow there'll be fifteen more," Connie said.

Glory sighed. "Max, how well did you know Tom?"

"He's from around here, you know. And then we were in basic together a long time ago," Max said. "We ended up in different units but managed to keep in touch over the years. He still has relatives here in Vermont so when he comes to visit he calls and drops by. He's been in sales for quite a while although he seems to frequently switch the companies he works for. Travels a lot. Not exactly sure what he's been selling lately. He was always kind of vague about his work. He was engaged to be married once but for some reason it didn't work out, and he never really wanted to talk about it. He seemed happy enough being a bachelor. When he called me last week, well, Connie and I decided the two of you might hit it off."

"I always enjoyed having Tom stop by," Connie said. "He was a nice guy, could be a lot of fun. Always polite, knew how to behave like a gentleman." She paused thoughtfully. "Sometimes over this past year he did seem a little distant at times, but you know how men can be. Women aren't the only ones who get moody. Anyway, Max and I decided Tom needed to have an evening out and you did, too. We certainly would never have set you up if we'd any idea . . . well, you know what I mean." Connie shook her head. "I have a tough time believing someone actually wanted to kill Tom."

"Yeah, doesn't make any sense," Max said, studying his beer bottle. "Guess it just shows we never know people as well as we think we do. I never would have guessed Tom had an enemy in the world." He finished off his beer, stood, and took the empty bottle to the sink.

"Any idea how Tom would have known Ron?" Glory asked.

Max puckered his brow and ran his fingers through thinning hair while he thought. "I don't remember that he did know Ron." He gave a little shrug and sat back down. "But this is a small town. Maybe Tom got a speeding ticket or struck up a conversation with Ron over a sandwich at the diner."

"Why do you say he knew Ron?" Connie asked.

"When I told him I had been married to Ron Lockhart, the chief of police, he said, 'So, you're *that* Lockhart.' At first he said he didn't know Ron personally. But then later, on the Ferris wheel, he said 'Glory ... I have to admit something.'"

"He had to admit what?" Connie leaned forward.

"Maybe he got a speeding ticket or something like that?"

"Well, then he said something really cryptic. He said, 'I didn't realize the hole I'd dug for myself until just now' and added that he *did* know Ron. I think he wanted to say more but, well, he didn't get a chance."

The kitchen phone rang and Max got up to answer it.

"Probably another nosey parker with more gossip. If this keeps up I'm going to take the phone off the hook," Connie said with some heat.

Glory could just imagine Gladys Prior and her cronies burning up the phone lines about how Glory not only went on a date with a man, but she chose a man who got himself shot in the back. Wagging tongues would ask if she had learned nothing from all those years of marriage to Rainbow's End's chief of police.

Glory thought about how her sons would handle the news. Tyler, of course, would have to deal with the personal side as well as the professional side. Thank goodness Glory got along well with his wife, and fortunately, their little boy wasn't old enough to understand his grandmother had gotten herself into the middle of a scandal.

Meanwhile, Cameron, along with his wife and their two kids, were on a vacation out west and wouldn't be back for another week and a half, so they would be out of this particular loop unless one of the other three boys got hold of them. Chance was on a date of his own this evening, and old enough that he wouldn't likely be home until very late. That left Joey, the baby of the family, home alone. He had just graduated from high school this spring and had gone out tonight for pizza with friends. He didn't have a curfew now that school was out, but Glory knew he wouldn't stay out late. She needed to be home when he got there. Heaven knew what he'd heard already.

"What's wrong?" Connie asked Max, who'd just hung up the phone, in a voice that pulled Glory away from thoughts of her sons.

"That was Bob Johnston. He tried calling your place, Glory, and figured you'd be here with Connie when he didn't reach you. He wanted to share what the authorities know so far."

Connie held up a hand. "Let me get us a glass of tea or lemonade first. What'll it be, Glory? Or I have some nice wine. Want a glass of cabernet?"

Glory turned to Max. "What do you think, Max? Does Bob's news call for wine or tea?" she asked.

Max patted her shoulder. "I'd say you've been through enough this evening that a glass of wine might do you good regardless of what Bob had to say."

Connie went to the cupboard for glasses while Max fetched the bottle of red wine. He poured each woman a glass before filling them in on his conversation with the medical examiner.

"So, they have indeed identified Tom as the deceased. They're in the process of tracking down family. I gave Bob the names of the upstate relatives. One brother and one sister that I know of. There, of course, may be others but if there are, Tom never mentioned them."

Glory took a sip of her wine. The feeling of sadness she'd felt earlier was back. Tom had been alive one minute and dead the next. So quick. So quietly gone.

Max continued recounting his conversation with the medical examiner. "The cops tried to clear the area as fast as they could but with so many people swarming around before they even arrived at the scene, it's difficult to find good, solid evidence. They do know one bullet pierced the back of the Ferris wheel cart and entered Tom's back. When the wheel started around for the last time, the cart the two of you were in would have been very close to the ground, so it would've been easy enough for someone to get a shot off. As the cart ascended a few more feet it would still be easy to pop a bullet into the back of the seat. It does appear from the bullet hole that whoever shot the gun would've been pretty much in a straight line from the cart."

"Wouldn't it be difficult, though, for someone to stand in the midst of all the people moving around and not be seen? Or heard?" Glory asked.

"One would think so," Max answered.

"There are disguises though, right?" Connie cut in. "You know what all you see at carnivals. There was a rodeo earlier today. Wouldn't look out of place to see a gun-toting cowboy or two walking around. Not to mention some of those attractions like the spooks from the haunted house or the freak show people."

"Or the clowns," Glory added, remembering she'd spotted a clown by the Ferris wheel.

"All of those might be good enough cover for someone shooting from the ground," Max agreed. "The other possibility is that the shooter had climbed up one of the structures located in the same area as the rides. The authorities are looking at those now. If a person could climb high enough, he could have gotten a straight shot into the cart when it was almost to the top."

"Whether shooting from ground level or higher, someone would have to be a pretty good marksman, wouldn't he?" Glory asked.

"Pretty good or pretty lucky. And I don't think whoever did this relied on luck," Max said.

No, Glory thought to herself, whoever did this was as good a shot as Tom had been. Someone who could shoot five duckies in a row without breaking a sweat.

Chapter 3
by Jennifer Vido

The rumor mill churned at top speed the next day as the various residents of Rainbow's End took liberties in adding their own particular spins on Tom's unfortunate demise. His reputation as a sharpshooter added to the exaggeration, for some believed he may have orchestrated his own death as part of a covert mission. Glory called hogwash on the absurdity of these tall tales, dodging neighbors and acquaintances as she went about her business in town. Her so-called date with Tom was apparently far from over. Her proverbial dip in the dating pool had turned into a royal belly flop for all to see.

Glory entered Glory Days through the back door in hopes of avoiding curious onlookers. Townsfolk milled about her storefront in search of a mere glimpse of the woman in question. Glory had been summoned by Chief Walker to the station at ten o'clock sharp to rehash the chain of events from the prior evening. With the store scheduled to open at nine that left approximately an hour or so for Glory to prep for the busy day ahead.

The annual sidewalk sale coincided with the county fair, which always drew people to town from the neighboring areas to join in the festivities. Competition remained fierce among the shopkeepers who vied for the honor of being named the most patriotic store in town. Glory had decided to recycle her red, white, and blue decorations from last year's prize-earning window display and add some updated bursts of stars and stripes with ribbons rather than design something brand new. She felt confident her store would be in the running for the coveted blue ribbon. Her sharp eye for design was the envy of her peers. Most owners spent the better part of the year planning and strategizing for the legendary Fourth of July contest. To be called the most patriotic on Main was a big deal.

"Escaping the heat or avoiding the swarm of bees buzzing about out there?" asked Lilly, Glory's sales assistant. She paused from sorting red sale tags just long enough to take a peek through the drawn blinds. Familiar faces assembled in small groups within plain sight of the store. Fingers were pointed in their direction as lively conversations ensued. No doubt the murder was the topic of conversation for all who gathered.

Glory heaved two reusable shopping bags onto the counter alongside a scattered pile of mail. "Don't they have something better to do this early in the morning? I wish they would scat like cats. How am I going to decorate the window display and gather items for the sale in a couple of hours?" Her questions didn't warrant a response. These were more like general statements highlighting the need to get busy in order to leave as quickly as humanly possible.

"I'll be sure to stay out of your way!" Lilly informed her boss.

"Thank you, Lilly. I don't know how I'd survive in this business without you."

Her trusty employee manned the place whenever Glory needed to be elsewhere. A member of the Jenkins clan, the young woman's familial history was evident around town. A hospital wing, an interactive playground, and even a historic monument depicting Rainbow's End forefathers boasted the family's name. Married with school-aged kids, Lilly worked part-time at the shop even in the summer months. With an abundance of local extended family, she experienced little trouble in rounding up someone to watch her kids. A lover of all things antique, her keen sense for original pieces contributed to the success of the business. If it weren't for her desire to work limited hours, Lilly would have been named manager of the store a long time ago. For now, she preferred a less defined role with plenty of flexibility.

As was common on any given day, Glory vacillated between selling and keeping rare antiques newly acquired for the store. Part of the beauty of owning an antique shop was having the inside track to find exquisite pieces not readily available to the public. Ron used to tease her endlessly about this very thing. Oftentimes she'd take an heirloom or two home after work and live with them for a few days, but eventually, they would return to their rightful places in the shop with some gentle prodding from Ron. The businesswoman side of Glory took seriously the need to turn a profit, especially since Ron's passing. Yet as a collector of *objets d'art*, the yearning to possess finer things had a way of tugging at her heart.

"Lilly," she called, "would you mind grabbing the end of this folding table? I'd like to set it up outside before I leave. One less thing to do when I get back from the police station."

"Are you sure you want to expose yourself to the masses?" Lilly teased.

Glory nodded and then propped open the front door with a worn, leather trunk. "If we move swiftly, I'll be able to get in and out of here without being accosted."

The two lugged the table through the glass door and to the sidewalk in one fell swoop. Passersby cleared the way as the two women positioned the trunk to the right of the store's entrance. Glory slipped back inside to grab a patriotic tablecloth to liven up the display, along with a couple of paperweights to hold it down. As she stepped back outside, she lingered a moment before completing her task. The light breeze carried scents of summer blooms, most especially the sweet fragrance of hydrangeas.

"A fine day for a sidewalk sale," bellowed a familiar voice.

Glory spied her oldest son sitting in the driver's seat of his squad car as it idled by the curb.

"Good morning, Tyler!" she shouted back. She stepped a few paces towards the naked table only to be intercepted by Lilly.

"I'll take these." Lilly gently removed the tablecloth and paperweights from her boss's hands. "If you don't go talk to that handsome policeman, I will," she joked.

Glory cracked a smile and headed over to the car.

"Hop in," said Tyler. "We don't want to keep the chief waiting. He's a busy man."

Glory checked her smartwatch. "I have at least an hour and then some until it's time to leave. I promise I won't be late. Lilly needs help with assembling the display, and the storefront needs my personal touch to get ready for the contest."

Tyler hesitated.

"Hurry along, son!" Glory insisted. "You're blocking the flow of traffic. Meet you there soon," she promised.

With that settled, Glory got back to work on the sidewalk display while firing off a list of things to be done during her absence. Mid-sentence she stopped. A young woman—a twenty-something wearing a distressed baseball cap—was peeking around the corner of the bakery, snapping pictures in Glory's direction. Wasting no time, Glory grabbed hold of Lilly's arm and ushered her back into the shop.

"Did you see what just happened?" she fumed. "Since when did I become a target of the paparazzi?"

"When you hang out with a dead man, your popularity has a tendency to soar," Lilly quipped.

"Duly noted," Glory replied with a hint of sarcasm. "C'mon. Let's focus on the task at hand. I need to wow the townsfolk and all those visitors with my carefully curated antiques. Why don't we take a look-see at what we have in the back room? Oh, and could you please grab that pile of mail on your way? You can sort through it while I'm busy wrestling with which pieces to include in our red tag sale."

The pair hunkered down in the storage room amid boxes and numerous crates filled with valuable antiques. There was no rhyme or reason as to where things were stored. Basically, as soon as something was acquired, it either made its way to the floor, Glory's home, or in here, depending on how much room was open for displays. Glory sifted through the smaller pieces taking note as to how long they had been part of the inventory. Lilly took charge of the mail, separating bills from inquiries from collectors and larger stores looking to unload overflow merchandise.

As Glory perused the stock, she came upon a large cardboard box marked *Fourth of July*, that had been shoved into the corner. Curious, she opened the dusty flaps and began pulling out the crumbled newspaper and bubble wrap.

"Whatcha got there?" asked Lilly. Pushing aside a pile of half-opened envelopes, she made room on the square folding table.

With gentle precision, Glory examined the box's contents. "This is exactly what I need for the front window. You can't get any more patriotic than this!" As she unwrapped each piece, both women oohed and ahhed over what she had discovered.

"These are ancestral muskets from the Revolutionary War. Look at the workmanship on these guns!" she said.

Lilly moved in for a closer look. "I can only imagine what famous patriots used these weapons to fight off the British. I bet these pieces would fetch a hefty sum."

Glory nodded. "These are one-of-a-kind finds that deserve to be displayed for the townsfolk of Rainbow's End to enjoy."

"Are they available for purchase or are these another one of your 'no sale' pieces?" Lilly never minced words. Unlike her boss, she rarely got attached to the inventory.

Glory ignored her comment because her focus had shifted to another item that had been tucked into the corner—an old telescope. "As a child, I marveled at the wonder of telescopes. I'd peer through the barrel for hours on end sometimes." She ran her finger along the cool brass, picking up a layer of dust. "Being able to see wide and far through a long scope like this one piques my interest. I bet the history buffs in town will feel the same. In fact, I predict this collection of rarities will fly off the shelves. Don't you agree?"

"Townies in Rainbow's End are fond of trinkets and pieces of history like these," Lilly agreed. "The old coots at the diner like to brag about their finds while discussing the day's news."

"I couldn't agree more," Glory said.

The pair worked side by side for the better part of an hour making significant progress. They arranged the boxes in an orderly fashion and separated what needed to be dragged out front. When the timer pinged on Glory's smartwatch, alerting her of the pending appointment with the chief, she dusted off her hands. "Would you mind finishing up for me, Lilly? I need to head over to the station. I don't want to be late. I'd never hear the end of it from Tyler."

Lilly didn't answer. She'd finally gotten back around to sorting the stack of mail, and was looking intently at a manila envelope. She flipped it over and peered inside.

"Lilly? Did you hear what I said?" asked Glory.

"Um, you may want to see this." Lilly handed her the envelope. Glory's named was scrawled across the front in black ink.

Glory raised an eyebrow. Placing a pair of cat-eyed readers on the bridge of her nose, she carefully opened the flap and removed a wrinkled piece of yellowed parchment paper.

"Where in the world did that come from and why did someone send it to you?" Lilly wondered.

Now it was Glory who didn't answer. She was concentrating on the document in her hands. She read and then reread it, being careful not to damage the fragile paper before looking up at Lilly. "It's a deed to a parcel of land in Queen's County. Says right here it backs up to the river and includes access to the water. If I'm reading this correctly, the property belongs to a Winifred Scott Ashford. Two hundred acres is a substantial tract of land."

"What about the other thing in the envelope? There's a bluish slip of paper in there as well," Lilly pressed.

"Let me see." Glory peered into the manila envelope and pulled out the paper. "It's a cashier's check made out to Winifred Scott Ashford for the sum of ten thousand dollars!" she exclaimed.

The pair stared at the check in disbelief.

"Anything else?" Lilly nodded at the envelope. "I didn't get a very good look in there."

"I can only imagine!" said Glory, looking inside.

Sure enough, there was a crisp white note card down in the bottom of the envelope. Glory read the words aloud.

Dear Glory,
I trust you will deliver this to Ashford. The life of someone close to you depends on it.
Tom

"This is unbelievable!" said Lilly. "It's from Tom? The same Tom from your blind date?"

Lilly's words faded in Glory's ears as she felt a sudden chill run up and down her spine. Tom dead, and now a mysterious envelope hand-delivered to her store? There was danger here—and the mere thought of her sons, or their families for that matter, being in the path of that danger made Glory shiver.

Ten o'clock couldn't come soon enough.

A hearty knock on the front door brought Glory back to the present moment. Time for the store to open, which meant customers and nosy neighbors trickling in with their questions, asking whether or not the rumors were true. A quick exchange between Glory and Lilly transpired—followed by Lilly cheerily welcoming customers into the shop, while Glory slipped into the back to tuck the envelope and its contents safely into her purse. For now, she decided to put it out of her mind. The sidewalk sale needed her attention. There'd be plenty of time to hash out the who, what, where, and why of the envelope with the chief and Tyler.

Glory's breezy attitude with the customers hid the anxiousness she felt inside. Pointing out additions to the inventory, she steered the customers away from the murder investigation and zeroed in on the upcoming sidewalk sale.

The owner of the nearby toy shop popped in, looking harried—her white hair flying and her cheeks pink.

"Cynthia! What brings you in today?" Glory asked.

"Kaleidoscopes!" Cynthia stopped to catch her breath. "My shipment has yet to arrive, and the children just love them. I ran an ad saying they'd been restocked, and now this delay!" She let out an exasperated sigh. "Any chance you have any antiques that I might borrow to tide me over? I just need something to put on display as I take orders."

The mention of kaleidoscopes brought a memory to the front of Glory's mind. "The last time I spotted one was at the fair. Actually, I believe I stepped on it. Long and thin. You may want to check in with one of the vendors at the county fair. You may luck out and find a booth with some to spare."

"You're a lifesaver, Glory," said Cynthia.

The two women hugged and compared decorating ideas for their store windows. Their conversation came to a halt at the sound of Glory's cell phone buzzing. A quick glance at the screen revealed her son's smiling face. "That's Tyler. It must be time to go. I need to grab my purse and skedaddle."

Glory crisscrossed her way through the store, trying hard not to get caught up in any unwanted conversations. Her son prided himself on being on time—or even being a little early. Being late to the meeting was not an option.

"Good luck!" shouted Lilly over the steady hum of the customers.

Glory waved goodbye and blew Lilly a kiss. The two shared more of a mother-daughter relationship than a boss-employee one, and Glory was grateful that she could rest her mind knowing that the store was in good hands.

As soon as she turned the key in her car's ignition, her heart started to beat faster. This whole situation was nerve-racking. With the envelope tucked in her purse, she made the short drive to the police station, located at the corner of Main and Elm. The redbrick building sat on the corner facing Mallard Park, which was a gathering place for locals, its charm and appeal for all ages making it a favorite spot in the community. Glory noticed a group of school-aged children playing on the new swings and slide while their mothers gathered in the gazebo, catching up on the day's gossip. She parked the car at the curb alongside the sandbox, which was currently occupied by a set of toddler twins.

Glory inserted a quarter into the meter. One hour would surely be enough. After all, what was there to say to the chief? Her knowledge of Tom Rankin and his death were so limited. Adjusting her outfit, she paused to breath in the smell of fresh-cut grass, then hurried inside.

Despite the recent murder, the station seemed awfully quiet. Glory approached the administrative assistant sitting behind the counter. The girl appeared to be in her twenties and was fixated on her cell phone. Glory waited a moment to be noticed, but the girl seemed to be engrossed in some YouTube video. Glory cleared her throat.

The girl hit the pause button and looked up. "May I help you?" she asked, seemingly unaware of her rudeness.

"My name is Glory Lockhart. I'm here to see Chief Walker for a ten o'clock appointment."

The girl consulted the computer screen for a moment and then replied, "Please take a seat. He's running a bit behind." She propped an elbow on the counter. "His wife called and asked him to pick up some milk and eggs because they have company. He only lives six blocks away, so it won't be too long. Please feel free to help yourself to a cup of coffee, and I'll let you know when he arrives."

Glory started to thank the girl for her hospitality, but a call came over the radio demanding her attention—something about a lost boy at the park.

Glory found a seat in the waiting area, opting to forgo the coffee. The last thing her jittery nerves needed was more caffeine. Instead, she tried to get comfortable in the government-issued chair in the corner, where she could witness the day's goings-on.

She heard a familiar voice and turned to look at the front door. Tyler and Chief Walker were just coming in, laughing and clearly enjoying each other's company. As they neared, Glory stood and waved hello.

"Well hello, Glory!" said the chief, wrapping her into a friendly embrace. "Thanks for meeting us here this morning." He chuckled. "Your son has quite the sense of humor. I assume he inherited it from you."

"I like to believe so," she answered with a twinkle in her eye.

As the chief ushered them down the hall, a little boy brushed past with a telescope in hand. Before Glory could think to wonder what the child was doing in the station, the toy slipped from his grasp and landed on the cement floor just underfoot. The boy turned back when he realized what had happened.

Glory quickly leaned over to retrieve the toy, and the sight of the long, thin object triggered the memory of stepping on something similar at the county fair, not far from the Ferris wheel. A jolt shot through her body as the vision sharpened in her memory. She realized it hadn't been a child's kaleidoscope she'd stepped on, as she had originally thought. Standing there in the hallway next to her son, everything suddenly became abundantly clear.

The object in question that ill-fated night was, she believed, a discarded rifle scope.

Chapter 4
by Laura Shea

"Glory, please, have a seat."

As they arranged themselves around the chief's desk, Glory noticed that Ned Walker's tone carefully balanced the personal and the professional. It was not just that he had served under Ron Lockhart, and that this was his widow seated beside her eldest son—who just happened to be his right-hand man. Glory knew that Ned had genuinely admired her late husband and had learned a lot from him. Part of Ron's legacy was apparent in Ned's interviewing style; he knew when to push the accelerator and when to pump the brakes. Glory had a feeling that most of this ride would be in neutral.

Ned asked Glory to begin whenever she felt ready.

"Where do you want me to start?" asked Glory.

"At the beginning," said the chief with a slight smile. "How did you meet Tom Rankin?"

Glory offered a concise summary of her time with Tom Rankin. That she had been fixed up on a blind date by her dear friend Connie, whose husband Max knew Tom back in basic training, and the two men had kept in touch through the years, if only from a distance. That at first Tom said he knew *of* Ron Lockhart, then admitted later that he knew him. That Tom was a sharpshooter and had won her a large stuffed teddy bear, which was now in police custody.

The irony that the sharpshooter had himself been shot was not lost on the chief, who showed little reaction beyond a slight raising of his eyebrows. Tyler glowered through most of the interview, his reaction much easier to read. Like the chief, Tyler had admired his father, idolized him, really, and Glory could think of no better role model. But unfortunately, Tyler had taken the lessons a little too literally, as he did almost everything else.

"If you don't mind my asking," Tyler began, after a brief nod from the chief, "do you remember him saying or doing anything unusual? Beyond what we talked about at the fairgrounds last night."

"Mostly, no," said Glory, turning her attention to her son. "We covered the usual getting-to-know-you stuff. I mentioned my four sons and three grandchildren." Tyler winced a little at this. "But he said very little about himself. Max told me later that Tom never married, although there was once a fiancée, but that didn't work out. When we were up on the Ferris wheel, there was something more Tom wanted to tell me about knowing Ron, but he didn't get the chance. He saw someone or something on the ground that scared him. He started shaking, then slumped in his seat. When I looked down, I thought I saw someone running away, but our carriage was too high up, so I can't be sure. Definitely can't describe him or her," she finished, anticipating Tyler's next question.

Although this was far from an inquisition, Glory felt that she was being asked not only to explain the details of her evening but also to explain herself, to justify the fact, at least to Tyler, that her life was going on after her husband's had ended. She was fairly certain that the official mourning period in Rainbow's End had elapsed, but if her oldest son had his way, she would dress in a permanent shade of black—not her best color—and lock herself away from the world. Glory knew she would miss her husband for the rest of her life, and even now, some days were harder than others. But she also knew that Ron would want her to live her life, especially after his had been taken so abruptly. Even in a small town, risk is a given when you're on the job as a police officer. People die in the line of duty and on the other side of that line. Glory just never expected it to happen to Ron—that danger would land on her own doorstep, and that it might be making a return visit now. Tyler certainly seemed to think so.

"Although I only knew him for about an hour, he seemed to be a nice guy," Glory said.

"Nice guys don't get shot for no reason," Tyler replied through gritted teeth.

"Your dad did, Tyler," Glory said calmly. "It can happen."

She knew this would touch a nerve. The chief knew this too and chose to move toward ending the conversation, at least for now. They could always pick it up another day.

"Anything else you can recall?" he asked Glory.

"Well, I'm sure your men have searched the grounds, but I stepped on something not far from the Ferris wheel. At the time I thought it was a child's toy, a kaleidoscope maybe, but now I think it was a rifle scope."

The chief and Tyler exchanged glances but said nothing.

"One thing more," Glory said, reaching into her shoulder bag and carefully extracting the manila envelope. "Lilly Jenkins found this in the morning mail. It was apparently hand-delivered to the shop."

She reached across the chief's desk and hand-delivered it herself. The chief's expression never changed as he emptied the envelope and surveyed the contents. Tyler rose and stood over his shoulder, reading the short note from a "Tom" with the implied threat to Glory's family, or possibly her friends, and then the cashier's check made out to one Winifred Scott Ashford.

This was more than Tyler could bear, and he exploded. "He expects you to do his dirty work for him? You barely knew him!"

The chief's professional calm remained unruffled. After all, it was not *his* mother a dead man was threatening if she did not act as his courier. While Tyler fumed, the chief quietly asked, "Do you have any ideas about this?"

"Absolutely none," said Glory, looking at her son and willing him to calm down before she had to invoke maternal privilege.

"Tyler . . . Ty," she began, using the childhood nickname that her son had demanded she dispense with when he was eight. "Are you okay?"

"I'm fine," he said, and it seemed to be almost true, as the anger in his face seeped away. "Are you?"

"Also fine," she said. "Truly, I am. You don't have to worry about me," she added, with more meaning than his question had elicited.

"So, Tom never mentioned any of this?" Ned waved a hand over the papers on his desk.

"No," said Glory. "As I said, he offered very little information about himself. Nothing about this."

"I see," Ned answered, deep in thought. "Well, thank you for coming in, Glory," he added, as if this had been more of a social call than a police interrogation, even one as gentle as this. "We appreciate your time. And we may have some follow-up questions . . ." His words drifted off as the contents of the envelope again claimed his attention. As Glory rose from her seat, so did the chief, remembering his manners.

"You know where to find me," Glory replied. "At home or at work," she said, secretly hoping that Tyler might sit out the next interview—if indeed there was one.

"I do," said the chief, nodding as she turned to leave.

"Do you need a ride?" asked a concerned Tyler, who had regained his composure but was still his mother's son.

"I drove myself, Tyler," she reminded him. "Give my love to Jen and Ronny," she said, exiting the room while exchanging a look with the chief. No explanations were needed. After all, he was a parent too.

During her drive back to the shop, Glory tried to focus on the road, but her thoughts kept returning to the events of the previous night—and those bled into the events of the morning. She had woken her two youngest sons, Chance and Joey, much earlier than either would have liked, and explained to them what had really happened before they were subjected to the multiple versions ricocheting around town. Glory thought it wise to stick to the bullet points, repeating more than once that she was fine. Both sons had known that their mother was going out on a date, and neither seemed to mind. Though all the Lockhart boys looked out for their mama, these two were more caught up in their own lives. While they seemed to follow her narrative, she had the advantage of their drowsy state, and neither asked any questions. Before long, it was time for Glory to go to work and for them to go back to sleep.

Glory had decided to spare her son Cameron and his family the news of her disastrous date and its aftermath, leaving them to enjoy their vacation. Of course, she had no control over what Tyler or the other boys might say or do. She was thinking about this as she drove up to the shop and parked her car. Stationed outside was a young patrolman she didn't recognize. Glory presumed it wasn't the antiques he was there to protect, and she doubted that this was the chief's doing. More likely, he had acquiesced to her son's request.

The officer seemed to be enjoying the display of Revolutionary War musketry as much as the antique gun enthusiasts were, and joined the conversation at the display table as though he'd just happened by for some shopping. The young officer's mind may not have been on potential assailants lurking in the crowd, but at least he wasn't scaring off customers. Glory breezed by him as she reentered the shop. The afternoon was, blessedly, uneventful. The local gossips were too busy spreading their own versions of last evening to listen to hers, but she knew they would check in eventually.

Glory expected to find an empty house when she returned home that evening. Her boys had their own places to go and people to see. When their path did happen to intersect, it was usually around mealtime. Glory was always glad to share a meal or a conversation with one or more of her offspring, but dinner alone tonight seemed just the thing. She dropped her bag on the hallway table and went straight to the kitchen at the back of the house. She didn't have much of an appetite, so her plan was to assemble a light summer salad while nursing a medicinal glass of chilled white wine as she rinsed and chopped.

That plan went on hold as soon as she entered the kitchen. Seated in one of the kitchen table chairs was a male figure, his back to her, his head bent forward. Glory had seen enough slumped male figures to last her a lifetime, so her first reaction was to scream. Of course, the only person to hear her was the strange man in her kitchen, who had been sleeping and awoke with a start. Jerking his head around, he turned to her, and she saw a face she knew only too well.

"Cameron!" she said. "What are you doing here?"

"Just thought I'd drop by," her second son answered with a slight smirk.

"But how did you know?" she asked.

"Captain Ty to the rescue, of course. He called last night. It was my idea to come back, although I don't think that's what our Ty had in mind." Cameron smiled as he said this. Tyler may have wanted to be rid of his childhood nickname, but Cameron didn't care. In extreme cases, he even reverted to calling him Ty-Ty. Cameron had always known exactly which buttons to push to annoy his older brother.

"But Cameron, your vacation," Glory said. "You should be enjoying time with your family, not babysitting your mother."

"That'll be the day," said Cameron. "Melissa and the girls send their love. I told them I needed to see Nana, but that I would be back soon. When Melissa got all the details, she put me on the first plane to Boston, and I got a rental car for the ride to Vermont. That's the rental parked on the street, in case you wondered."

Glory had been so preoccupied with her own thoughts that she'd failed to notice the car parked in front of her house on a street where everyone parked in their own driveway. She would need to pay more attention to her surroundings, she reminded herself, until all of this had blown over.

"And while we're at it, the key under the flowerpot in the back?" Cameron shook his head. "Really, Mom? *Still?*"

"You have keys to my house, Cameron."

"Yes, I do," he said. "It's just that I don't take them with me on vacation. And I wanted to get here as soon as possible, so I didn't stop at home first. Might I suggest that you find another hiding place?"

"I could," said Glory, "but then your younger brothers might be locked out on a regular basis. So I think we'll keep things as they are."

"Suit yourself," said Cameron.

Glory dearly loved all her sons, but she and Cameron understood each other in ways that often made the words redundant. Tyler thought he knew best when it came to his mother, but Cameron knew better.

Always a strong student, Cameron had gone away to college, then on to law school. Glory had fully expected that his future lay in a big city, so she was more than a little surprised when Rainbow's End became *his* rainbow's end. He had married his high school sweetheart, who had hung on through all his years of higher education. Melissa was a local girl who would not leave her mother, and Cameron would not leave Melissa, so he commuted to the most prestigious law firm within driving distance. They seemed very happy with each other and their two girls, for whom Glory, the mother of sons, could not buy enough pretty dresses, even when their parents begged her to wait at least until their birthdays.

"So, how are you?" asked Cameron, trying to sound nonchalant.

"I wish everyone would stop asking me that," said Glory, a little annoyed. "I'm fine."

"Wouldn't have it any other way," said her son.

"Tom Rankin is the one who people should be concerned about," she said.

"Tom who?" asked Cameron.

"Rankin. The man I met last night." She paused. "Please don't tell me you knew him."

"Don't think so," said Cameron. "Who is—was—he?"

"He was a friend of Connie's husband, Max. They went way back, although Tom didn't live around here.

You know how everyone knows everyone in this town—"

"Don't remind me," Cameron interjected.

"*And* their business," finished his mother. "Well, Tom didn't. Although he did say he knew your father but didn't get a chance to say how before—"

"I see," said Cameron, sparing her from recounting any more painful memories. "It's just that—"

"What?" said his mother. "You *did* know him?"

"I didn't, no," said Cameron. "Dad might have, if it was the same guy. Probably not."

"Tell me anyway," Glory insisted.

"Okay," said Cameron, "but really, it's a long shot."

Glory took the seat next to him as he began.

"It was years ago, I was maybe nine or ten. I managed to insert myself in between Ty and Dad for once. Even then Ty was his right-hand man."

"Your father had two hands, Cameron."

"Maybe," said Cameron, "but it didn't always seem that way to me. Anyway, my break came when Ty went away to camp. For a couple of weeks, I got to be Dad's wingman. It was a Saturday afternoon, and Dad asked me if I wanted to go for a ride with him. He had to meet a man about a—I don't remember what—but about something. I was only too happy to go, especially after being consigned to the back seat whenever the three of us, the Lockhart men, went anywhere.

"We drove for a long time, at least it seemed a long time to me, to a place out of town that I didn't know and couldn't recognize now if you asked me. There was a man there, who lived in a small house, by himself. I remember being a little disappointed that there wasn't a boy there my age, or any kid, or even a dog, to play with. Dad and the man went inside the house to talk and left me to amuse myself on the front lawn. Luckily, they weren't in there for very long, and when Dad came out, he and the man shook hands and that was it. Back in the car. On the way home, I thought Dad said the man's name was Reynolds, Raynor, something with an R. Rankin, maybe. It was a name I hadn't heard before and a place I'd never been. It's probably not the same guy."

Cameron looked directly at his mother. "Dad said we were on official business, and we couldn't discuss official business with anyone. I thought this was totally cool and promised to say nothing. Which I never did."

Seeing his mother's unease, Cameron finished his story.

"But the coolest part, and probably the only reason I remember this, was the ride back. It started to rain. In buckets. Dad kept on driving, and he let me stick my arms out the passenger window until the rain got so bad, I had to close it. I got drenched, but it was great while it lasted. I remember thinking that this was the difference between my father and my mother. My father would let me stick my arms out of a car window in a full-out rainstorm, and my mother wouldn't."

"Your fondest childhood memory," said Glory, a little hurt.

"Don't worry, Mom. I would never let my girls stick their arms out of a moving car window, whatever the weather. I'm my mother's son to the last. I promise."

Glory touched him lightly on the arm. Sensing her relief, Cameron quickly broke the mood.

"So, Mom," he asked, "what's for dinner?"

Chapter 5
by Emma Pivato

Glory did a quick mental review of the contents of her fridge and realized that she'd forgotten to defrost anything for dinner—not surprising after all that had happened. But she did have a few vegetables including a large bag of fresh spinach and a jar of pesto, and cooking was one thing Glory could do well. Soon, she and Cameron were sitting down to quite a respectable meal and she found that her appetite had returned with the pleasure of his company.

"This is delicious!" Cameron said between mouthfuls. "I don't remember you making it when I lived at home. What is it?"

"It's just pesto pasta but I doctored it up a bit."

"*Quite* a bit, I would say. What exactly did you do to it? I bet Melissa and the kids would love it!"

"Oh." Glory said, embarrassed. "It's really nothing special. Joey is resisting eating meat lately and with his heavy sports schedule I worry about his limited protein intake so I supplement protein where I can."

"Okay, but what's in it?"

"Well, the base is fusilli pasta, as you can see, but it's made out of chickpeas. And the sauce is just jarred pesto from Costco—it's an excellent product, with wholesome ingredients, even though it's from a jar," Glory added. "I put about four cups of washed spinach leaves through the food processor until they were in little pieces and then microwaved them for about a minute. I also chopped up a red pepper and three leftover green onions that I needed to use up and microwaved them for just thirty seconds. Then, I added everything to the fusilli pasta after it was drained and threw in a tablespoon of sliced green olives and about a cup and a half of feta cheese. At the end, I mixed in pesto sauce to taste, and that's it. Simple!"

"We are definitely going to have this at our house, even if I have to make it myself!" Cameron said. Glory smiled happily. He had always been the quickest of her four boys to compliment her cooking, and she'd missed that. They still had dinner together fairly often, of course. But it was good to have just Cameron here for a meal, so the two of them could catch up.

Roasted tomato halves crusted with a mixture of panko, dried basil, lemon pepper, Parmesan cheese and olive oil had accompanied the pasta. Avocado halves with lime quarters had preceded it, and homemade rhubarb coffee cake, quickly defrosted and warmed up, had followed.

After supper, they moved to the living room to enjoy their tea and Cameron sat back, looking comfortable and happy. But he also looked very tired from his long flight. He shook himself as though to stave off any thoughts of a nap and turned to his mother. "Okay, Mom. Tell me from the beginning exactly what happened. I had Tyler's version but now I'd like to have yours."

Glory told him about the blind date Connie and Max had arranged for her and how she'd met up with Tom Rankin under the Ferris wheel. She was about to go on when he interrupted her.

"I'm happy you were ready to date someone, Mom. Dad wouldn't want you to spend the rest of your life alone. I'm so sorry about how it worked out, and I hope this won't stop you in the future from dating."

Glory looked at her second oldest son fondly and realized for the first time how much she had been hurt by Tyler's criticism. "Thank you for saying that," she said softly and patted his hand. "Now, where were we?" She sat up straighter, her mind feeling clearer.

When Glory got to the part about the hand-delivered note coming to her shop, Cameron interrupted again. "I'd really like to see that note. I can't believe Chief Walker and Tyler just took it from you. It contained a threat to our family. They should at least have made you a copy as a reference. And a copy of that check, too."

"Oh, I'm not that naïve," Glory said. "After all those years with your father, I know how the police operate." She pulled out her phone. "I snapped pictures of all three items before I went to the station, but I haven't had a chance to look at them yet." She scrolled through and found the photos and handed the phone to her son.

"The note's a little blurry," he said, squinting at the phone. "I wonder if your friend, Max, would be able to identify the handwriting from looking at it, assuming he's had any correspondence from this Tom person?"

"Are you thinking that Tom might not have written the note?" Glory asked, surprised.

"Well, consider the situation. Since he died last night he would've had to deliver the note yesterday, before he'd even met you. Does that make sense?"

"I don't know. Maybe not. I mean, it's possible, I guess."

"When does your mail get delivered at the store?"

"Around noon—but Lilly usually brings it in. I don't remember what happened yesterday because we were very busy with customers all day and trying to decorate the store and get ready for today's sidewalk sale at the same time. All I know is that previously—"

"You need to find out what time Lilly brought the mail in."

"Yes, but how will that help?"

"If we can narrow the timeline, it will be easier to check if any of the neighbors saw a person other than the postman putting something in your mailbox before then. And the police could check video footage from store cameras in the area as well." After a pause, Cameron went on. "There's something else that needs to be looked into. Whose bank account was that check drawn on? It's signed by the cashier and guaranteed by the bank. Tyler will have to try to get that information from the manager and he'll probably need to get a subpoena first."

"But what about the threat? Who made it? It seems to me that's the most urgent matter to deal with," Glory said.

"Where are Chance and Joey?" Cameron asked suddenly, a twinge of alarm in his voice.

Glory felt panic rising in her chest. She hurried to the phone. To her relief, Chance answered right away and told her he was spending the night at a friend's house. Glory didn't ask for details; she was just relieved that he was safe. Just as she hung up, the front door opened and Joey walked in. He was happy to see Cameron but looked preoccupied. "I'm going upstairs to make a phone call, Mom. I may be down later."

Cameron watched him knowingly. "Girl trouble, I bet," he said after Joey had headed up the stairs.

As Glory and Cameron both sat back to relax, Glory realized that her heart was racing. "We can't just sit here," she blurted out, turning to Cameron. "Maybe we should call Tyler!"

Cameron looked at her, the lawyer part of him at war with the son part. The son part won out. "No," he replied. "This is not the time for worrying about correct procedure. That'll take forever. The person we're going to call is this Ashford." He opened his phone to pull up the Rainbow's End directory. "What was the name on that paperwork, again?"

"Winifred Scott Ashford."

Cameron scanned the names in the listing. "There's no listing for her, but there is one for a Scott and Elise Ashford. Should we try that?"

"I wonder if Winifred is a man's name, and he goes by his middle name, Scott."

"A man named Winifred?" Cameron looked skeptical.

Glory chuckled. "Well, I know it's unusual, but some older men have been named Winifred."

"Let's just call and find out what's going on before it gets any later," Cameron said.

Glory put a hand on his arm. "Tyler's not going to like it if we interfere with the investigation. Neither is the chief. And you're a lawyer, Cameron. Couldn't you get in trouble for this?"

Cameron considered her words for a moment. "Mom, I know it's true that any interference in an ongoing police investigation *could* be deemed unprofessional conduct by a lawyer—and I guess it's possible I could be disciplined or even suspended." Cameron went on to explain that his qualms were trumped by his concern for his family's safety. "Look," he said finally, "the letter came to you, Mom. It contained a deed to a property you don't own. Surely the right thing to do is to let the owner know that you have it in your possession. You make the phone call." Before Glory could protest, he added, "If I'm ever reported to the law society I'll say that I advised you *against* making the call. Is that better?"

"I can live with that," Glory said. She dialed the number and put the phone on speaker. "Hello," she said when the phone was picked up. "My name is Glory

Lockhart. Am I speaking to Mr. Winifred Scott Ashford?"

"Yes. What do you want?"

Glory started to explain but was quickly interrupted. "What do you mean you have the deed to my property?" the man bellowed.

She started to elaborate, but Cameron handed her a hastily written note that read, "Don't mention that Tom is dead." Glory continued with the rest of the story and ended by asking him if he knew Tom Rankin.

"Never heard of him," Ashford snarled.

"Well, then how would he have gotten hold of your deed, and why would he be sending you a check? Maybe your wife knows. You could ask her and…"

Ashford interrupted her. "Elise? She left me three months ago! The deed was in our safety deposit box at the bank. Maybe she took it!"

"Did you acquire the property after you were married?"

"Yes, but…"

"I think under communal property law, unless your wife specifically signed away all claims to it, you own it jointly." Glory looked at Cameron inquiringly as she said this, and he nodded his head in agreement.

"No *way!*" Ashford yelled into the phone. "My grandfather left me that property in his will. I was his namesake. That's how I got that gawd-awful first name, Winifred!"

When Glory said nothing, he added plaintively, "He was *my* grandfather! Elise has no claim to that property."

"I guess you'll have to discuss that with a lawyer," Glory said, soothingly. "I'm no expert, and I may be wrong. But do you have any idea why my family would be involved in any of this? Why would Tom say that someone in my family would be at risk if I didn't get the deed and check back to you?"

"I have no idea. I just want to get my deed back. When can you get it to me? I can pick it up tomorrow if you live here in town."

Glory explained that she'd turned everything over to the police, and this was met by a string of invectives from Scott. When he finally ran out of steam, she went on. "If I could just talk to your wife maybe we can find out what the connection is between my family and yours. Can you please tell me where to find her?"

"I haven't a clue! I don't keep track of her these days. Are we finished here?"

Clearly, they were. Glory knew it was pointless to prolong the conversation. "Thanks. I'll let the chief know how to reach you."

Ashford grunted and hung up. Mother and son discussed the phone call for a few minutes. Cameron looked at Glory and asked, "So when did your friends set this date up for you, anyway?"

"Tom apparently got into town on the weekend and Connie asked me Monday if I'd consider it. I agreed then, so I'm sure she got in touch with him shortly after. It was her idea that we meet at the county fair and that just started yesterday."

"Well, we can ask Max and Connie more about that tomorrow and also about the handwriting on the note. I don't think there's anything more we can do about the situation tonight."

The next morning, with Cameron in agreement, Glory called the chief directly to report what she'd done, but she made sure to leave Cameron out of the conversation. She'd decided it would be easier to talk to Ned than to try talking to Tyler. She realized that she was still quite angry with her son for his judgmental attitude toward her.

Ned Walker was not pleased that Glory had taken it upon herself to contact Mr. Ashford, but he understood her need for action given that her family might be under threat. He promised to follow up on tracking down Ashford's wife, and to tell Glory what he could once they found her.

Two hours later, Glory was at her shop, inventorying what was left over from the sidewalk sale when the phone rang. It was Ned. "Elise Ashford was found dead two hours ago, about the same time we were talking," he told her tersely. "The coroner says she died between five and seven this morning. We're bringing the husband in for questioning."

After the call, Glory felt a sudden wave of overwhelming guilt. She excused herself to Lilly and ran to the back room. She sat down at the table with her head in her hands. *Is Elise Ashford dead because of my phone call to Scott Ashford?* She asked herself this question over and over, actually muttering it out loud.

Suddenly, she felt gentle hands on her shoulders and raised her head to see Tyler, looking at her—this time with compassion instead of judgment. "Don't blame yourself, Mom. We were planning to tell Ashford the same story today and ask the same questions as you did last night. So, if his reaction really was to kill his wife after he heard what he heard, he could just as easily be doing it tonight as last night."

Glory looked at him in surprise. This was a new side to her son that she hadn't seen before—at least not lately. And what he said made sense. She'd only relayed to Ashford the same facts that the police would have.

At that moment, Lilly stuck her head timidly in the door. When she saw Glory's smile, she came forward holding two iced coffee drinks from the Starbucks down the street. "I thought you could use these," she said softly. Glory and Tyler both thanked her and she left quickly.

When they were alone again, Tyler turned to Glory. "There's something else I need to say. I was wrong to make such a big deal out of you dating Tom, Mom. Dad has been gone a year now." Tyler's voice cracked when he said this. "You need to make a new life for yourself and you have every right to do so on your own terms. It was very wrong of me to add to your grief and upset by being so snotty."

Glory saw that Tyler's whole body was tense and she could tell it had cost him a lot to say this. *He must be mellowing with age,* she thought with a smile. Only later did she learn that his younger brother had had a good talk with him!

Chapter 6
by Joyce Oroz

Just three tumultuous days after Tom's murder, Glory had come to terms with her nerves, her fears, and her duty. Her duty was clear: protect her loved ones by finding Tom's murderer. Living in a family where police work was as natural as breathing, where Glory's husband and now her son Ty put their lives on the line every day in the service of justice, why shouldn't she use her brain, intuition, and maybe some luck to catch a killer? She had a few leads to follow and some people to talk to.

Glory arrived at her antique shop, and a moment later, Lilly's car pulled into the back lot beside hers. The ladies met up in the shop's backroom where a coffee pot sat at the ready. Minutes later, the crowded little cove off the main showroom began to smell like fresh perked coffee and donuts from the bakery.

"Lilly, you shouldn't have…." Glory swooned.

"You've had a rough couple days. I thought something sweet and gooey would help get your day started on the right foot," Lilly said with a smile.

"It'll help my day but not my waistline," Glory giggled. She hadn't giggled about anything in days and it felt good. "Lilly, I was wondering if you'd like to put in some extra hours here at the shop this week." Glory mentally crossed her fingers, hoping Lilly would say yes. "I have out-of-town business to take care of."

"As long as the kids are in school, I'm all yours," said Lilly. "I see what you're going through and I want to help any way I can."

Glory settled in at her desk chair and thumbed through yesterday's receipts while Lilly buzzed around the shop, straightening up various displays. The shop was due to open in half an hour, but someone was already peeking in the window.

When Glory realized who it was, she hurried to the door and unlocked it, admitting the patrolman who'd been guarding the place along with a gust of chilly morning air. The official police uniform didn't do much to hide the fact that the young man looked fresh out of the academy and was probably still more than a little wet behind the ears. But he was a friendly fellow and Glory invited him in for a donut.

"Ma'am, I just wanted you to know that there's some kind of graffiti out here."

"What?" Glory stormed out the door and stood with hands on hips ready to slug whoever had spray-painted a black spider onto a section of wall beside the large display window. Her body went cold as heat rose up into her face.

"Did you see anyone?"

"No, ma'am, I just arrived."

"I'm sorry, Officer—uh—"

He laughed. "I'm Ned Walker's little brother, Calvin."

"Calvin! Oh my goodness, you've grown into a very handsome young man. I remember when you were…oh never mind. Officer Walker, who do you think did this?"

"Actually, it's the only graffiti we've experienced in this part of town in years. So we know it's not a pattern. It's also not a gang symbol." Calvin rubbed his chin. "Seems very representational, like it's making a point— but I'm not sure what the artist was trying to say."

"Sounds like you'd make a good detective." Glory had an idea. "Have you ever thought about doing investigative work when you're off duty?"

"Never considered it, but I'm always looking for odd jobs to help pay off my student loans."

"That's nice to know. Could I get your number—or do you have a business card, maybe?" Glory asked, as Lilly appeared on the sidewalk beside them, her eyes widening when she saw the spider.

"Looks like we're decorating for Halloween ahead of schedule," she said in a small voice.

No one laughed. Creeped out by the spider, they moved inside.

Calvin handed Glory his card. "You can reach me at that number when I'm on duty. If you want, I can also give you my cell number."

"Great." Glory grabbed a pen from her desk and took down his number, jotting it on the back of the card. She wondered if the officers were allowed to take investigative work on the side, but what the heck—*it's a free country*, she thought to herself.

In the meantime, Lilly dug out the leftover exterior paint they kept in a bathroom cabinet. She carried the bucket into the showroom.

"Not yet, Lilly," said Glory, holding up a hand. "I need to call the chief first and get his opinion on this. And it wouldn't hurt to take a few photos of the damage before we cover it up." She felt a rising sense of dread in her stomach. "What if that graffiti is connected somehow to Tom's murder?"

"I see your point, boss. I'll set the paint aside until we need it." Lilly proceeded to straighten the bookshelf and then rearranged a large collection of antique salt and pepper shakers. She was trying her best to act relaxed, but Glory could see her jaw was tight, her shoulders tense.

The shop opened, and Calvin returned to his post in front of the building, pacing the sidewalk and stopping now and again near the entrance to do a bit of window shopping. Inside, Glory and Lilly made phone calls and waited on customers. At least half of Glory's business came from people looking for very specific items. If the desired antique was not already in her possession, she would typically add it to her list of things to search for online and in other towns and shops. She had planned to make the two-hour drive up to Middlebury that day, where there was a sweet little antique shop full of hard-to-find collectibles, but decided to put that on the back burner until after Chief Walker had checked out her spider.

When he arrived a short time later, he seemed both surprised and disappointed at finding graffiti in his town. He stood outside, conferring with Calvin for a time, then pronounced that he had no idea how such a thing had happened in Rainbow's End—on Main Street, no less. He finally left, grumbling something about some disgruntled tattooed teenagers from another town.

Glory quickly put her ducks in a row—making sure that Lilly would be able to stay at Glory Days until closing—and got ready to leave for Middlebury.

On her way out of town, Glory decided to stop off at Connie's house. Her best friend knew antiques as well as any pro, and might like to come along. She found Connie outside, working in her garden, and she was thrilled to shake off the soil and go upstate to hunt for treasure. She hoped to find a certain antique Tiffany bronze table lamp, and eat lunch at the Garden Restaurant while they were at it.

Heading out of town on Route 7, Glory filled Connie in on the latest news regarding the murder investigation. She told her about the note that had been delivered to the antique shop, and about her talk with the disagreeable Winifred Scott Ashford—and that the police had found Ashford's wife Elise dead and brought Ashford in for questioning. She ended by telling Connie about the latest—the mysterious spider that had been spray painted on the wall.

"Did it look like a black widow spider?" Connie asked.

Glory nodded. "Yes, I guess it did. Maybe that's why it looked so sinister and scary."

Connie thought for a moment, "I wonder if…."

"If what?" Glory asked, turning down the volume on the car radio.

"I'm sure it doesn't mean a thing—I just wondered if there might be a connection between you as a widow and, you know, a black …."

"Oh, I see what you're thinking. That would mean that it wasn't a random act at all. It was aimed to scare me specifically." Glory's voice slipped down to a whisper. A somber mood filled the car until Glory finally took hold of herself and turned the radio up again. A minute later, the two were singing along with the music and laughing.

Glory made a right turn. Connie looked at her, frowning.

"Glory, why are you turning off the highway? We're barely out of Rainbow's End."

"I looked up Winifred Scott Ashford's address and I wanted to see what the place looks like. After all, I had his deed in my hands until I gave it to the chief. The man sounded like a snooty old coot on the phone."

Connie asked Glory if she'd called Ashford to let him know they were coming.

"No call was needed," Glory assured her. "I just want to see the neighborhood. I don't know if I told you this before, but Lilly lives up in this area."

"Oh my!" Connie gulped, looking around them at the tree-lined lanes, gracious lawns, and fine homes. "I would love to live here. Every house is beautiful and the yards are huge! It looks like each one has several acres with it. And the maples are lovely the way they line the streets. Oh, look at the house up ahead. The stonework is incredible and the gables and ironwork. Look, Glory! Those stained glass windows must be lovely from the inside. Wish we could go in."

"The house you love so much is the house we're looking for: 27 Clover Circle." Glory parked her car across the street from Ashford's house and turned off the engine. The ladies gazed at the magnificent structure for several minutes; obviously it was the oldest house in the neighborhood.

Suddenly, a man wearing black Lycra spandex from head to toe sped around the back of Glory's car on a bicycle, making a sharp left across the street, and slowing to a stop halfway up the circle driveway in front of the beautiful house.

"Now's our chance!" said Glory, opening the car door.

"Are you sure about this?" Connie said, following suit.

As the rider bent down to check his skinny bike tires, the ladies scurried across the street and up the driveway. He heard them coming and looked around.

"Hello, Mr. Ashford?" Glory said, breathlessly.

"Yes, hello…" he muttered.

Connie waved a hand. "My name's Connie. Nice racing bike you have there."

"Yes, I believe it is. Tire's a bit low on air at the moment."

"And my name is Glory Lockhart…."

"Name sounds familiar," he grunted. "You wouldn't be the woman who's holding my *deed*?" His blue eyes scrunched into a squint as his middle-aged clean-shaven jaw tightened. He whipped off his cap and wiped his sweaty brow with the back of his hand. His hair had receded only slightly and had just a sprinkling of gray. He looked down at the women.

"I'd invite you in, but I'm not looking for trouble."

Glory held up her hands. "No worries! We just stopped by on a whim," she explained. "You sounded awfully gruff on the phone the other day and I just wanted to see what kind of person I'm dealing with. But now that I've met you, you seem like a reasonable fellow."

"And you look like a normal person—not someone who'd make up a crazy scheme like the one I heard over the phone. If your story's true, when am I going to get my deed back?" Ashford glared at Glory.

Glory sized him up quickly and decided he was all bluster. "As I told you over the phone, the police have the deed. They seem to think this craziness might be tied into Tom Rankin's murder. The note was signed, it would appear, by Tom." Glory shrugged innocently.

"That's hog-wash!" said Scott. "I inherited those two hundred acres, and I want my deed!"

"Your lawyer will have to work that out," Glory said, "but in the meantime someone is threatening to hurt someone dear to me, and I don't even know who."

Tom seemed to relax a little. "Would you ladies like to see my acreage in Queen's County—the acreage in the deed?"

Connie looked at Glory. Glory looked back at her. Finally, Connie suggested they take a look at the property, and Glory concluded it might help her to straighten out the deed situation. Besides, Queens County was in the same direction as Middlebury.

Within a few minutes, they were off. The ladies followed as Ashford got in a black Mercedes and drove eight miles north on Route 7, and then two miles west on Route 4. He eventually led them half a mile on a one-lane country road that turned out to be his driveway. He parked his car at the end of the drive in front of a small Disney-movie-like house with a peaked roof, shutters, and bricked path to the door.

"This is so cute," Connie said, as they clambered out of the car. "And look, there's a path down to the water."

The first thing Glory noticed was how quiet and isolated the tract of land was.

Ashford led the women down to a pier that had three sets of pilings knee-deep in the slow-moving crystal clear water. It was obvious that he had a childhood history with Otter Creek, judging by the way his eyes sparkled at the sight of his fishing hole. On one side of the creek was a long stretch of shade trees, mostly cottonwood with sprinklings of hemlock and hickory. The side they stood on had no trees. It was open to acres and acres of flat meadow land. The only structures in sight were the little Disney house and the pier. Who could ask for more?

Glory immediately felt an affinity for the river, the meadow, and the cottage. It reminded her of her childhood—it was almost as though she'd been to this place before. But, of course, that was a silly thought. After seeing the property, though, she could understand why Ashford was so anxious to get his deed back.

"Well, ladies, what do you think?" he asked, standing there at the water's edge, still dressed in his biking outfit.

"It's more than lovely," Connie crooned. "It's magical."

Ashford smiled knowingly.

"I'm at a total loss for words." Glory felt choked up. Something about this place deeply moved her. She cleared her throat. "I'm afraid we need to continue our trip to Middlebury now, but thank you for the tour." What she really wanted to say was, "Let's just stay here all day." But she had business in Middlebury and Connie wanted to rummage through antique stores.

Ashford led them across his property and onto Route 4, then back to the main highway, where he gave them a wave and turned south.

Glory accelerated onto the highway going north. After an hour and a half of smooth sailing, they reached their destination, the Garden Restaurant in downtown Middlebury. Located on a quiet side street, the Garden was the place to be. It had the best food and service in town, not to mention a spectacular floor-to-ceiling mural covering the entire length of one interior wall featuring giant colorful flowers. Some of the twelve o'clock working crowd had already left, leaving room for the one o'clock people, like Glory and Connie. As they sipped white wine and dipped crusty bread into seasoned olive oil, the subject of Max's relationship to Tom came up.

"Like I said, Max knew him from the service. They both made 'sharpshooter,' but I don't know what else they had in common. Just friendship I guess," Connie said, as the waitress placed a salmon salad in front of her.

"Max said Tom had been engaged, but he never married," Glory said, poking her fork into a plate of lasagna. "What happened to the woman?"

"She was a young woman—eighteen, I think, and her father disapproved of the engagement. Tom was brokenhearted and signed up for duty in Desert Storm."

Glory stared at her food.

"What's wrong? I thought you were hungry," Connie said.

"In the note, Tom said, 'I trust you will deliver this to Ashford.' Instead, I gave everything to the chief of police. It doesn't set well with me."

"You did it to protect someone. Wish we knew who that is," Connie mused. "It was good that you let Mr. Ashford know what was going on. He's not really a mean guy and he's not bad looking if you ask me."

"Yeah," Glory said, absently pushing a bite of lasagna across her plate with the fork. She took a sip of wine.

"The endangered person referred to in the note could even be you," said her friend.

Glory stared at Connie and wondered for the hundredth time what was going on.

"I've never seen you like this," Connie said, a worried look in her eyes. "Even when Ron died, you were such a trouper."

"Connie, would you mind very much if we went back to the little house by the river?" Glory's mind had not left the beautiful river for a moment. She felt strangely drawn to it.

"What? I thought…never mind. Finish your lunch and let's go to the river." She laid a hand on top of Glory's. "I can see that something is bothering you. Can you tell me what it is?"

Glory stared at her plate. "Why would Tom give Ashford ten thousand dollars? I mean, you saw his house and his country place. The man is obviously rich, unless he has huge debts or something…."

"Okay, my friend, let's get out of here. That lovely river will fix your mood," Connie said, giving their server a wave.

They paid the bill and drove out of Middlebury on Route 7 going south. Almost two hours later, they parked beside Scott's little Disney cottage once again. Connie followed Glory around the property as she poked around here and there looking for something, anything that would help answer her many questions. They sat on the pier, took off their shoes and dangled their feet in the cold stream.

Glory looked up into the trees across the creek. "Is that a tree house up there?" She pointed to a small section of weathered wood peeking out from among leafy branches.

"Where? I don't see anything," Connie said.

"See the tree with the speckled trunk? Now look above the first branches…."

"Oh! I see it now." Connie looked closer. "I think you're right, Glory, it's probably something kids built in the tree."

Glory was already rolling up her pant legs—which turned out to be a futile effort because the creek was waist-high.

"Glory, what do you think you're doing?" Connie yelled. "Wait for me!"

The two women plowed through the water and up the far bank. Soaking wet, they shivered under the long shadows cast by a sinking afternoon sun. Connie was ready to turn back almost immediately, but not until she could bring her crazed friend along with her. So off they went to the tree with the speckled trunk. Once they were there, Glory ran her hand over the rough bark, looking up into the foliage where the crude old treehouse appeared to have straddled three thick branches as it watched the years go by.

Glory felt some odd indentions under her fingers, and lowered her eyes to the trunk. She gasped at what she saw. "Connie, come here and look at this!"

Connie moved closer to the tree, wondering what Glory had found that would evoke such excitement.

Glory had her hands pressed together against the trunk. Slowly she pulled them away, revealing a heart that had been carved into the wood.

Connie did a double take. "Does that say what I think it says?"

"You tell me. Was Tom's girlfriend named Mary?" Glory asked in a hushed voice.

"You know, I think it was, but it was so many years ago...I can't be sure."

The women stood staring at the crooked heart surrounding carefully engraved letters. *TOM R. loves MARY A.*

Chapter 7
by Christian Belz

Glory traced the carving with her finger, felt the edge of the depression, smoothed with time. She imagined the knife cutting into the tree bark, the pressure of the fingers on the knife, the hand of the boy making the cuts, the girl on his mind. The carving on the tree transported her back in time, reminding Glory of her own teenage romance—the boy *before* Ron.

Students from Rainbow's End, like many of the smaller towns in the surrounding area, were educated in the larger school district a few miles to the north. Beginning in seventh grade, Glory had bumped along the two-lane blacktop on the daily bus ride to Mill River High. Each fall, she would meet a whole new crop of kids from towns which would occasionally join Mill River's outreach program.

Not a shy child—as a matter of fact, she could be downright outspoken—Glory was nonetheless a bit late, and somewhat awkward, in her development of relationships with boys. Not that she wasn't interested. It was simply that she hadn't had an older sister or close friend to help her along. So she was taken aback when Harrison, the new boy in her English class, approached her in the hallway one afternoon. Her hair was still damp from the shower after gym. Her mind was processing the volleyball strategies she'd learned as she opened her locker to grab the book for Spanish. When she turned, he was there. He started talking and honestly, she thought he was going to ask about their homework assignment, and was shocked when she heard the word *prom*. She had to catch her breath before answering. And then a big smile spread across her face.

This was some thirty-seven years ago.

Her mom and her Aunt Nellie had helped her sort through the available dresses in the church's basement sale. Most of the meager selections were dowdy looking, or pink. Glory hated pink. But then they discovered a shiny baby-blue dress. The fabric was not only a beautiful color, but it had a crispness to it, not like the other gowns on offer. It swept down below her knees, which she loved. But it was strapless, which seemed rather bold. She had never worn a dress like that before.

"Your date's going to love this!" Aunt Nellie said. Nellie worked part-time at the beauty salon in town, and asked if she could fix Glory's hair for the big night. She seemed excited about the prospect. "I've got something real special in mind," she said. It occurred to Glory then that maybe she could have looked to her aunt for boy-related concerns before this.

Aunt Nellie sectioned Glory's hair and used a device that looked like a big stapler to crimp it one section at a time. Then she swept half of it up, and left the other half to cascade over her bare shoulders. Glory looked in the mirror, turning this way and that. She looked so different! Next, Aunt Nellie helped her with her makeup. When Glory's mom saw her all dressed up, tears clouded her eyes.

As it turned out, Harrison was from Rainbow's End too, although Glory had never seen him around except in school. His family had moved to town halfway through the school year.

When he showed up at her front door on prom night, Glory knew the evening would be magical. The usually slightly nerdy Harrison had transformed into a prince.

He looked nothing short of dashing in his white suit and midnight blue bow tie. Glory's mom had them stand in front of the rosebush by the porch to take pictures, and then they climbed into her dad's car so he could drive them to the dance.

They sat quietly in the backseat, nervous as they traveled the familiar bus route to school. The crowded gym had been transformed with shiny black and white decorations, strings of twinkle lights, balloons, and streamers. Glory felt a surge of happiness.

Once the music started, she was able to burn off a bit of the excitement that made her knees jittery. She danced almost every dance with Harrison, but a couple of other boys from class asked her to dance as well, and she felt elated at being so popular! Glory and Harrison spent a little time at the snack bar, and halfway through the evening, he went over to talk to his friends, while she caught up with her girlfriends.

Toward the end of the night, the DJ played *Endless Love*. Glory's heart began to race when Harrison held out his hand and led her to the dance floor. He had just taken her into his arms when Glory's eye picked up a sudden movement to her left. A guy was rushing toward them, zigzagging around couples on the edge of the dance floor. She gasped when, instead of slowing down as he approached them, he lunged for her and grabbed her wrist.

"Hey!" Harrison called out, slapping his hand on the guy's shoulder.

Grinning, the guy shrugged Harrison's hand off, then grabbed Glory. She recognized him from chemistry class, a boy with a dark shag that flowed along his face. The one who always stared at her—made her uncomfortable. His name was Slade. Glory had heard he was from Ridgeville, the wild town to the north, known for its gun ranges that had earned it the nickname *Rangeville*.

Glory tried to pull her hand away from his grasp. "Slade! Leave me alone!"

"Don't you want to dance with me? We could make this our song. *Endless love!*"

She finally managed to pry her hand out of his. "No!" She turned to Harrison, who stood there in shock. She took his hand. "Come on, this song is for *us*." They walked out onto the dance floor, Harrison glancing back at Slade.

"Don't worry about him," said Glory. "Let's just dance."

The two of them swayed in a close embrace, Glory humming along with the song. But then she caught Slade's intense stare. He paced alongside the floor, his eyes not leaving hers. When he caught her looking, he laughed. Waved. Stuck out his tongue. She couldn't help but smile. She turned her head to hide it.

Three weeks later, they were together. Glory and Slade.

"Glory . . . Glory!"

"Huh?" Glory shook off the memory and looked at Connie, whose brow was wrinkled with concern. "Oh, sorry, my thoughts carried me away for a moment there." She took in her surroundings, felt the warm breeze, and refocused on the carving on the tree in front of her. "What is Tom Rankin's brother's name? Do you know?"

"Slade. I remember because it's an unusual name. There's a sister, too. Heather."

"Slade Rankin. That's what I thought." Glory chuckled and shook her head. "Small world. Let's go see him."

"Why?"

"I'll explain in a minute. He's a clue in all this. Do you know where he lives now?"

"Pretty close. He's in Clairville. I don't have an address, but I remember Tom mentioning that Slade owns a restaurant up there." Connie thought for a moment. "Now what was it called? Something . . . the name reminds me of a horse. Chestnut? No—I know! It's called Nutmeg's. That's it!"

"Hmm. How far away is that? Do we have time?" Glory stepped away from the tree. "I'd like to check this out while it's on my mind. On the way, I'll tell you all about Slade."

"You'll tell *me*? What are you talking about?"

Glory started walking back toward the creek. "Come on and I'll explain everything." She paused at the water's edge. "I'm not looking forward to crossing this again." She turned back to Connie. "Hold on a minute. Do you have your phone? I left mine in the car."

Connie nodded. "I grabbed mine just in case."

"Before we go, could you snap a picture of those initials on that tree? For the record."

Once that was done, they made their way back across the creek, and along the way, Glory filled Connie in on the prom and what had happened in its wake. "I lived to the south of school, Slade to the north. I didn't drive back then. My parents couldn't have given me a car, anyway—me or any of my three younger sisters."

Connie narrowed her eyes. "So let me get this straight. You and Slade Rankin ended up getting together—even after he'd pulled that shenanigan at the prom?"

"Yeah, well, Harrison was a very nice boy. Polite, responsible. Nothing wrong with that. But Slade . . ." Glory shook her head. "His confidence got my attention. He'd get an idea and just go for it. No hesitation. There wasn't anything he wouldn't try." She looked at Connie, who had stopped walking mid-stream and was standing there with her hands on her hips. "Don't look at me like that. Maybe I liked the bad boys back then, I don't know."

"Before you married a cop."

Glory grimaced. "Yeah, right." They walked on in silence for a few minutes more. "Slade. He would come to see me in his rusted out '68 Caprice. After school let out for summer, we'd explore the backwoods around where we lived. Slade had a minibike and we'd zoom up and down the dirt trails. My socks collected so much dirt! One trail we explored went pretty high up a hill and came out onto an overlook with a spectacular view of the valley. It was really beautiful.

"Once in while on the weekend we'd make a day of it and drive the two hours to the ocean. I loved sitting on the big slabs of rock and watching the waves and sea spray. So relaxing. And then there was target practice. Lord, we did a lot of target practice."

They finally arrived at the other side of the creek and picked their way up the slight incline, water dripping from their clothes.

"Let's rest for a minute," Connie said, pointing to the pier. "We have plenty of time."

The boards squeaked as they walked halfway down its length. They sat and dangled their feet into the water.

"Target practice? Really?" Connie said.

"There were several ranges in the area, but Slade and Tom's dad was a member at one of the larger ones. Slade loved his rifles." Glory stopped short.

"What?"

"His scopes; he had a couple of favorites. The range hosted these events. Slade took me to the egg shoot once, a competition where they set up five Grade A large eggs at the line for each person. With 45 rifles in the competition, it was something to see! Slade shot from 300 yards and hit eleven eggs over the three matches."

"Wow!"

"Yeah, he was a great shot."

They sat watching the creek, long shadows from the trees along the other side fluctuating with the rushing and rippling of the water.

"You did break up eventually. What happened?"

Glory sighed. "On Labor Day, my family and the next door neighbors planned a big picnic, over at Mallard Park. They invited everyone in both extended families. Whole generations would be there, from babies to at least one great-grandma. Barbecue, salads, sides, volleyball and games for the kids. And pies, my family made the best pies! You know, it would be the whole picnic experience. I wanted Slade to come. It would be a chance for him to meet everybody and we could relax and have some fun."

"It didn't work out?"

"He wanted me all to himself. Said it was our last few days together before school started, and the end of summer. He wanted to go camping in the woods. Just the two of us. I put my foot down. It was our first big argument. And our last, as it turned out. He tried to win me back after that, came around two weeks later with a big apology, a balloon bouquet, and a mix tape. But I wouldn't have it. I'd had time to think, and had realized Slade wasn't for me."

Connie nodded.

"There's something else. One time that summer, he helped me bake apple pies for a fundraiser. He noticed the color of the spice we were using matched my hair. He gave me the nickname *Nutmeg*. He called me that all summer long."

"Oh—wait, are you serious? Glory, he named his restaurant after you! After all these years!"

"We don't know that. But we should find out." Glory braced her hands on the pier to stand. "All right, are you ready?" When she looked at Connie, she noticed an expression of puzzlement on her face. "What is it?"

"Something's been bugging me."

"What?"

"Scott Ashford. He didn't seem upset *at all*. Didn't that seem strange to you? About his wife dying, I mean. He was out biking as though he didn't have a care in the world. Then, he brought us to this property. It hadn't occurred to me until now, but do you think it's possible that he hasn't been told about Elise's death?"

Glory thought about this. "Well, he certainly *should* know about it. Ned Walker called me right after they found the body yesterday morning to inform me, and mentioned they were bringing the husband in for questioning."

"Humph. So they brought him in. Well then, maybe after all that, he's repressing his feelings, trying to ignore them. Some people react that way to a death."

"Or maybe he just really hated his wife," said Glory. "Oh, that reminds me, Bob Johnston was going to track down and notify Tom's relatives that he'd died. If he did, Slade may already have made his way down to Rainbow's End."

It's A Small World interrupted them, emanating from Connie's pocket. "My phone!" She answered it. "Oh, hi, Tyler. Yes, she's right here." She handed the phone to Glory.

Tyler explained that he'd been trying to reach Glory and was worried when she didn't pick up.

"I'm sorry, Tyler. I haven't been near my phone for a couple of hours. I'm fine. I'm spending the afternoon with Connie."

"Okay, good," Tyler said, sounding relieved. "What have you two been up to?"

Glory explained her day trip—then came clean and told Tyler about stopping to see Ashford and the subsequent visit to his beautiful property.

"Mom! You shouldn't have gone to see him." Tyler's voice went up an octave. "This is police business and there's absolutely *no need* for you to take that kind of risk."

"I know, but we're fine. Actually, it's been a rather nice afternoon. We're out here by Otter Creek, and it's a beautiful day."

"You're still on Ashford's property? You have to get away from there! I don't want to have to come get you. Tell me you'll leave right now. Please!"

"It's okay, Tyler. We were about to go anyway. We'll be on our way within ten minutes. But we found something you should check out." Glory told Tyler about the carving on the tree and how there was a distinct possibility that the initials were referring to Tom and his fiancée, before their broken engagement. "I'll have Connie text you the photo she took."

After she hung up and Connie sent the picture, they put on their shoes and walked to the car. Once inside, Glory dug her phone out of her bag and called Bob Johnston.

"Yes," said the medical examiner in answer to Glory's question. "I tried to reach both Slade and Heather. I didn't get through to either one. Neither has returned my call."

Glory thanked Bob and asked him to keep her informed. She started up the car, and with one last glance back at the creek and the Disney house, headed north and proceeded onto Route 7. "Since neither of Tom's siblings have talked to Bob, they probably don't know he's dead."

"I wonder why they could neither one be reached. Maybe they're out of town, or tied up in some other way. Or maybe they don't respond to unknown callers. A lot of people don't."

"Once we get to Nutmeg's, at least we can see if Slade is there. I want to put my eyeballs on him, and find out what's going on." A nervous knot grew in Glory's stomach. So many years had passed. Was the name of Slade's restaurant just a coincidence? She had a feeling it wasn't. But what had he been thinking when he'd chosen the name?

The sky turned from blue to pink as the sun set, streaming bright rays through the evergreens to their left. Traffic wasn't too bad. An occasional car or truck passed them going southbound, while a good number of trucks were on the northbound side. Glory drove only a few miles above the speed limit. In her rearview mirror, she noticed a navy blue sedan behind her, keeping a respectable distance. At least he wasn't riding her tail.

Connie looked up the restaurant on her smartphone and started the GPS function. They listened to the woman giving them directions in an English accent. Soon she advised them to turn right on River Road.

"I was tired of the American woman telling me what to do," Connie said. "It's so much easier to take directions from a Brit."

Both women laughed at this, but after the turn, Glory stopped smiling. There was the blue car again, staying behind them. "I think we're being followed."

Connie turned. "I saw that car at the Garden Restaurant in Middlebury, too. I remember, because it had that green parking sticker in the window."

Glory glanced in her rearview mirror. "Oh, you're right!"

"See that motel up ahead? Pull into the lot, and we'll find out for sure."

Glory parked right next to a flashing VACANCY sign at the motel, which was situated across the street from a combination gas station/diner with a huge canopy in front. When she'd pulled off the road, the blue sedan had continued on past. Glory made a big sweep through the motel lot, and found a parking spot facing the road. "Let's wait here for a minute."

A short while later, the blue car came back their way and drove into the gas station on the other side of the street, backing into a spot by the restaurant.

"That confirms it," Glory said. "Now I have to call Tyler."

Chapter 8
by T'Gracie and Joe Reese

Glory found it difficult to press Tyler's name into her smart phone. Her hands were shaking.

Calm down, Glory, she told herself. *So there's a blue car across the street—so what? That isn't a reason to be terrified. There are lots of blue cars in the world, and there might be a perfectly reasonable explanation for the fact that this one seems to be following us. And look at Connie. She seems calm. You should be, too.*

Continuing to reassure herself, she finally managed to call Tyler.

He answered quickly. "Mom, where are you?"

She told him, and his response was immediate.

"Get home!"

"It's all right, Tyler. We just—"

"It's *not* all right. Get home. Now. You're with Connie?"

"Yes."

"Then both of you come home. Do you want me to come get you?"

"No, of course not."

"Then come home without making a single stop. Do you understand? Hang up the phone. And come home. Now."

Glory agreed that she would head back to Rainbow's End and clicked off the call. "All right," she said to Connie. "We probably need to—"

Before she could finish her sentence, the phone buzzed again in her palm. Probably Tyler again, calling to make sure they were on the way. Glory swiped the 'answer' button.

"Tyler," she said, "I've already told you, you don't have to—"

But it wasn't Tyler. Instead, a raspy voice hissed, "Nutmeg. Come to Nutmeg's."

The phone went dead.

It took them five minutes to reach the restaurant from the motel parking lot.

Connie was dubious. "This may not be such a good idea, Glory."

"We don't have too much of a choice."

'Of course we do. We can go home, just like Tyler told us to. You don't even have the slightest idea who was on the other end of that call."

"I know exactly who it was. It was Slade."

Connie looked doubtful. "He said two words and you know who it was?"

"He said *four* words, but yes. And the truth is, he wouldn't have had to say anything at all. He could have just breathed, and I'd recognize him. That's how I always reacted to Slade."

"But Glory, look. The restaurant is closed!"

It was. And it had been for two weeks, or so the sign said. No mention of a reopening date.

Nutmeg's was housed in an old frame building. Its windows were dark as a tomb, save for the twinkling in the big front windows—a reflection of the few summer stars that had popped out early and the round-as-a-dime full moon that was rising in the summer Vermont sky.

Glory and Connie got out of the car and walked to the door.

"It's got to be locked, Glory. We can't just…"

Glory tried the door, and it swung inward, squeaking slightly on its hinges.

"Damn," whispered Connie.

"Come on."

"What makes you so brave all of a sudden?"

"Insanity."

They walked past the deserted reception area, the darkened cash register staring silently at them as they made their way through the bar, then into the restaurant's main dining room.

"So what do we do now?" whispered Connie. "Order the soup?"

"We sit down. That's what you do when you go to a restaurant. You sit down."

"Yes, but usually you're not alone in the building, and usually the restaurant is not haunted."

Glory chose a table and pulled out a chair. The scraping sound echoed across the room.

Connie had just seated herself when a figure appeared at the top of a staircase which led upward to the darkened second floor.

The figure, bent and gaunt, moved slowly so that it almost seemed to be gliding, but one by one it negotiated the steps, until it finally crossed a patch on the stairway that was illuminated by moonlight.

Glory could not suppress a gasp. "Slade?" she whispered.

Was that a smile on his face?

It was to be fully half a minute before she was certain—half a minute before the figure stood beside them, looking down at them, coming as close as it would ever again come to what had once been a smile.

"Slade Rankin?"

"My Nutmeg."

These words were breathed rather than spoken. Slade's face was pale in the dim light—a face that had once been so vital, so scornful, so confident.

Connie had been right. This place that had apparently once been a restaurant was now haunted, and the ghost inhabiting it now hovered over the two of them.

That hiss again. "Want to go shooting, Nutmeg?"

"Slade!" She heard her own voice speaking his name, and in her ears, it could well have come from a Glory of many years ago—a girl in high school talking to a boy in chemistry class.

A Morning Glory who no longer existed, of course, but who, despite the years, had not suffered what he had. What had happened to him?

"The '68 Caprice is gone, Glory."

"Yes. I know."

And even though she knew the pain it would cause, she could not help asking, "What has happened to you, Slade?"

A slow shaking of the head. "Life did. And they did."

"Who? Who do you mean by *they*?"

But Slade Rankin could not answer, his eyes having become fixed on something or someone he seemed to perceive coming through the door:

"Tom is dead," he said.

"I know that."

"He thought he could beat them. I knew he couldn't. Now I'm dead, too. They're here. They're coming in."

"There's no one here, Slade."

He had on a stained white sport jacket, and he kept reaching into its pockets, fingers fumbling for something that was not there.

A gun?

It didn't matter. Because whatever he saw, or thought he saw, bullets would not affect.

With great effort, Glory diverted her horrified gaze from his horrified gaze so that she could glance, if only for a second, at Connie's horrified gaze.

She wanted to reach across the table, grasp Connie's hand, squeeze it, and say reassuringly, *It's all right! It's going to be all right!*

But of course in that moment, Glory wasn't sure it *would* be all right, ever again.

Slade looked down at her. "You'll be dead too," he said, almost in a whisper. "If you don't give it to them, you'll be dead too. Only they'll make it more horrible for you. You're so beautiful. I don't want to see you suffer." He grimaced a little, as if feeling a stab of pain. "Give it to them, Glory."

"What? What do I give to them?"

"It isn't worth trying to keep. You can't hold onto it."

"What, Slade? What are you talking about?"

"Listen to me, and remember. Remember what I'm going to tell you now. Will you remember?"

"Yes. Yes, I'll remember."

"You must lie down where all the ladders start. In the foul rag and bone shop of the heart."

"I don't understand that." Glory was starting to feel frantic now. Why was Slade speaking in riddles? "I don't understand what you're trying to tell me."

"I know. I know you don't understand. But I do. I know about the land, and the deed, and the check. I know about them and I know about your son who thinks he can be the man your husband was and keep all the laws and help all the people. And I know about your other three sons and how much you love them. You don't want to be in a world without them. But you will be. Unless you do as I tell you."

"How do you know these things, Slade?"

He shook his head. "Do you hear them? They're coming. They can come down through the roof. But only at night. You don't have to be afraid of them during the day. That's how they deceive you—they look like the flowers. You think they're the flowers. And then night comes!"

He bent lower then and put a hand on her shoulder.

In an instant, she remembered dancing with him, his hand on her shoulder.

"You must lie down where all the ladders start, Glory of the Morning. And you have forgotten to do that."

"All right. But how do I do that?"

"Think. When did it all start for you, Nutmeg? When did the killing begin?"

And Glory did think. "The fair. The Ferris wheel."

A slow nodding of the head.

"Do you know about the fair?" Glory asked. "And how Tom was shot?"

"Oh yes. And that's where you must begin. That's where you must go back to. You saw people under that Ferris wheel, didn't you? A clown. A man smoking."

"Yes. But how did you…"

"And how many people had a gun?"

"No one."

"How many people gave Tom a gun?"

Slowly, beginning to understand, she said, "One. The man in the booth."

"That booth, Glory. A booth with rifles already in it. Toy target rifles, of course, but how hard do you think it would be to smuggle in a real rifle? A deer rifle, let's say."

"So are you saying that the man in the booth shot Tom?"

"I'm saying that someone in the booth could have shot Tom, and no one would have noticed. So that leaves one character in your little drama that everyone has overlooked. He went to jail—but no one questioned him. He's *still* in jail, and no one questions him. No one analyses him—no one even thinks about him at all. And he is where all the ladders start!"

"But Slade, no one went to jail! No one.." And then Glory had another thought. "The only one who went to jail was my stuffed bear. And, as far as I know, he's still there."

Slade nodded, but then appeared frightened again. "Go and find out what the bear has to tell you. You'll have to go at night. That's when they come out, so you'll have to be careful. Don't you have a key to the jail that your husband had before he…"

"Yes. It's an old set of keys. It's still in the desk."

"Then go where the ladders start! Goodbye, my Morning Glory, my beautiful Nutmeg!" With that, Slade turned and made his way up the stairs, never looking back.

Then, on the top step, a tall and willowy woman appeared. "You need to go now."

"Who are you?" asked Glory.

"You need to go now."

"All right. But one question: who wrote these words about going down where all the ladders start?"

"His name was William Butler Yeats. But…" The woman shook her head. "But he's dead too. So it doesn't matter."

Then she, too, disappeared.

Glory and Connie got up and walked to the door of the restaurant. Upon reaching it they heard high-pitched sounds from upstairs.

They couldn't tell if the sounds were crying or laughing.

Chapter 9
by Trisha Durrant

They drove back to Rainbow's End in silence. Connie huddled in her seat, leaning against the door, as far away from Glory as she could get. She was still trembling, and Glory knew it was her own fault.

Ron had always told Glory she was too impulsive—reckless he called it. *I should never have gone to that restaurant—especially after dark*, she told herself. The guilt was compounded by the fact that she'd dragged her friend there as well. But the temptation had been too great. Once she recognized Slade's voice, she simply couldn't wait to see him again. But to see him like that! What had happened to change the handsome, risk-taking boy she had loved all those years ago into a grotesque, pathetic shell of a man who could barely navigate a flight of stairs?

Something darted in front of the car, and Glory slammed on the brakes. Connie screamed.

"It was only a rabbit," Glory reassured her friend. She decided to put all thoughts of Slade away and concentrate on driving. She had never driven too well after dark.

Despite her best efforts, once she was back in the rhythm of the tires rolling over the tarmac, the events of the day came flooding back, unbidden. Meeting Scott Ashford, following him to the disputed property in Queen's county, wading across the river to see the carved heart and Tom Rankin's initials, along with those of the mysterious Mary A. The disastrous visit to the restaurant which had so terrified Connie. *Why had she never known that Slade had a brother and a sister?* Glory asked herself that question for the hundredth time. And what was the significance of Tom's reaction to her last name and the fact that he had known that Ron had been police chief of Rainbow's End?

And Slade! His paranoia, his cryptic remarks about 'lying down where all the ladders start'? Death had started with the bear, he said, and she should visit him at night. The bear was in the evidence locker at the station. She could see it anytime. All she had to do was ask Ned—so why did she have to go at night?"

They were coming into town now. Connie's house was ahead on the left. Glory pulled into the driveway and Connie had the door open before she'd even come to a complete stop.

"Goodnight," she called, but there was no reply as Connie scuttled up the driveway and disappeared onto the porch. Glory waited until a light came on in the house before backing out of the driveway and heading for home.

When she arrived, it was to find the house empty. She stumbled up the stairs, and her last thought before she fell into a dreamless sleep was to wonder who the tall, willowy woman in the restaurant was.

The next morning there was no time to mull over the events of the previous day. The fair was in full swing and Glory knew the day ahead would be a busy one.

As she was going out the door, Cameron stumbled down the stairs. "Hi, Mom; sorry I didn't get up earlier. I'll be at the store soon. I figure with the fair you'll need extra help. I thought I'd man the outside table for you."

Glory went back and gave him a hug. "Be sure to eat a good breakfast. It's usually a madhouse with no time to stop for anything."

When she got to the shop, crowds were already starting to gather. Lilly had the coffee made and had already stopped at the bakery.

She grinned at Glory. "Let's get the table set up outside then we can take our coffee break and have one of those delicious doughnuts."

Glory took one end of the table, and Lilly took the other, and together they wrestled it through the door. Glory covered it with the cloth while Lilly went back inside and started bringing out the boxes of merchandise.

Glory was smoothing the creases away when an angry voice thundered in her ear. "What did you do to Connie last night? She won't tell me what happened, but it'll be a cold day in hell before I let her go anywhere with you again."

Startled, Glory looked up to see Max Robertson looming over her. "I'm sorry…"

"The hell you are!" He stomped off down the street before she could even attempt an explanation.

"Mom, what was that all about?" Cameron was staring down the street at the man he used to call *Uncle Max*.

He turned to Glory and she quickly said, "Something happened yesterday when Connie and I went on a road trip to look at antiques. I'll tell you later. Right now, we've got to finish setting up."

Cameron, Lilly, and Glory worked without a break until closing time. It wasn't until Glory and her son were together in the kitchen at home that she was able to answer his question.

He listened in silence, his face grim. "So you went to a deserted restaurant after dark to see a man who you briefly dated in high school, and his behavior was so bizarre that Connie was freaked out?"

Glory nodded. Put that way, maybe it hadn't been the wisest decision she could have made.

"And now Max is angry with you?"

"I didn't know Slade was going to be so weird." Even to her ears that sounded like a lame excuse. "All I really wanted to know was if he knew why Tom had sent that packet to me."

"Did you find out?"

"No; he quoted some poem, but I haven't a clue what it means."

Cameron picked his cell phone. "Tell me as much as you remember."

"*You must lie down where all the ladders start. In the foul rag and bone shop of the heart.*" Glory shrugged. "That's all I remember. The woman who was with Slade said it was by William Butler Yeats ."

Cameron looked up from his phone where he had been busily entering the words. "Found it. Irish poet. Considered one of the greatest of the twentieth century. Those are the last lines of his poem called, *Circus Animals' Desertion.*"

"But that still doesn't tell us what Slade meant by it."

"And since I studied law not literature I'm no help." Cameron paused. "Ty tells me you also visited Scott Ashford."

Glory sighed. "Yet another of my bad decisions today, according to your brother." She couldn't help thinking of Ashford's behavior. "Scott must have been notified of his wife's death yet he didn't seem upset in the least. He talked as if she were still missing. Then he even took us to the property mentioned in the deed and let us look around."

The steely glare Cameron shot Glory told her he agreed with Ty's assessment. "Mom, you've got to leave this alone. This is best left to the police department."

Glory agreed with him—well almost.

Later that evening, the phone rang. Glory was already in bed and would have let the call go to voicemail except the caller ID said it was Connie, so she picked up.

"Glory, I'm sorry for the way I behaved yesterday," Connie whispered. "It was... Anyway, I'm sorry and I'm sorry about what Max said to you. He's not been himself since Tom was killed. I remember hearing them talking soon after he arrived. Tom was saying the same things Slade said about letting them have it or they would come for them..." Connie broke off. Glory heard her hurry across the room, then the sound of a door closing. She came back on the line. "I don't want Max to hear us talking but that's why I was so terrified. If it had been just Slade saying those things, I would have figured he was simply crazy, but Tom had said the same things to Max, and now he's dead."

There was a moment of silence, then Connie went on. "I've been thinking about the carved heart and the initials. In all the years I knew him, Tom never mentioned his fiancée's last name. Max told me she came from a prominent family and they objected to the relationship. Do you think it's possible that the *A* stood for Ashford?"

"You mean she could have been Scott Ashford's sister?"

"Maybe. I mean, it sort of adds up. We were on the Ashford property, which had been in the family for a long time." Connie paused. "Is there any way we could find out without asking a lot of questions, do you think? I want to keep things discreet from here on out."

Glory had two sons who disapproved of her meddling in the case, so she was inclined to agree with Connie. "I know someone who might be able to tell us."

"Who?"

"My assistant, Lilly Jenkins. She was an Evans before she married, and these old families know everything about the people in their social circles. I'll ask her first thing in the morning."

And she did, but she didn't get the answer she'd expected.

Chapter 10
Owen Magruder

Glory fell into bed for another fitful night's sleep. She awoke with a start around five a.m. on Friday morning. If her scratchy throat was any indication, she had been screaming in her sleep. The bedclothes were damp with perspiration and she was trembling and chilled. Her heart was pounding like a hammer. Only the sunlight filtering through her bedroom window told her *yes*, she was home and *yes*, she was in her own bed. Slowly, as the fog of slumber lifted, she realized with relief that she had been dreaming—a horrid, terrifying nightmare having something to do with a ghoulish-looking Slade and the shuttered Nutmeg restaurant. *Well*, she thought, *I'd best pull myself together and get down to the shop. Maybe Lilly and her family's long history here will help me make some sense out of the past forty-eight hours. Some breakfast will do me good, too.* Her feet on the cold bedroom floor snapped her fully back to reality.

Meanwhile, William Steele and his partner, Joe Sherman, drove straight from their office in Rutland to Chief Walker's office in Rainbow's End.

The administrative assistant looked up from her cell phone and flashed a smile. "Can I help you, gentlemen?"

"Like to see Chief Walker." Steele's reply was curt and to the point.

"And you are?"

Steele and Sherman both handed over their FBI badges.

"Oh, I see! Just a moment. I'll get the chief for you." She exited into the office behind the counter and soon returned with Ned Walker in tow.

"Gentlemen, what can I do for you?" He ushered them into his office, motioned to two chairs in front of the desk and closed the door.

"We're here about the Rankin case. I assume you're the lead investigator."

"So far, yes. What do you need to know?"

"Everything you have so far. From the top." Steele was true to his name—always got right to the point, never minced words, rarely showed much in the way of emotion.

Chief Walker nodded and brought the two agents up to speed. "Rankin was visiting friends here in town who arranged a date for him with Glory Lockhart, widow of the former police chief, Ron Lockhart. The couple was riding on the Ferris wheel when Rankin was shot and killed."

"Weapon?"

"We don't know for sure but we assume it was a pistol."

"Not a rifle?" Steele asked.

"Not likely. The medical examiner says the bullet was a nine millimeter."

The agents nodded in understanding. There weren't many made rifles in that caliber.

"Besides," Chief Walker continued, "can you imagine someone firing at the Ferris wheel with a rifle from the fair concourse and nobody noticing? In addition, the shooting gallery is in front of the Ferris wheel and Dr. Johnston, our medical examiner, says the bullet came through the back of the gondola seat and stopped in Rankin's heart just behind the sternum."

"Angle?

"Dr. Johnston said it was a slightly downward angle. That means the shot would have to have come from a position above the gondola Rankin was in. The Ferris wheel was on flat terrain and there are no tall buildings or hills where the shooter could have been hiding. No, most likely a pistol. Death was pretty quick. According to Mrs. Lockhart, he made no sound, but just slumped in his seat and that was that."

"Sounds like someone in the gondola above Rankin's," Steele observed.

"That's what we think," Walker confirmed.

"Shell casing? Suspects?" It was Sherman who spoke this time.

"I have to admit, we didn't look for casings. Assumed it was a rifle until Dr. Johnston retrieved the bullet. By that time it was too late what with all of the people milling about. And the Ferris wheel company started breaking down shortly after we removed Rankin's body. As of now, we have no suspects. None."

"What about the woman with him—Mrs. Lockhart?"

"Like I told you, she's our former chief's widow. Glory's one of the nicest people around. Pillar of the community. No, I don't think she's a likely suspect."

"She was the last to see him alive, wasn't she?" Steele asked.

"Yes, well, eh. . . ."

"Chief, we have to consider all possibilities," said Sherman.

"I know that, but Glory . . ." Chief Walker was beginning to take offense at the line of questioning. This was, after all, his case, or at least so he thought. "And what is the Bureau's interest in Tom Rankin?"

Steele and Sherman exchanged glances. "He was one of us."

"You mean he was an agent?"

"Precisely. You see, this case is both professional and personal to us," Steele said softly. "We'd like to talk with the Ferris wheel's operator, Dr. Johnston, Mrs. Lockhart, and the other people who were on the Ferris wheel at the time. Where can we find them?"

"I'll get my receptionist to give you Dr. Johnston's and Mrs. Lockhart's phone numbers and addresses, but the Ferris wheel company closed up shop that night and went to their next fair, St. Albans, I think it was."

"You didn't impound the wheel? Call in the state forensic team?"

"Didn't seem worthwhile. There were hundreds of people milling about."

"But one of those people killed Tom Rankin!" Sherman raised his voice this time.

Steele quietly put his hand on Sherman's arm and said, "Chief Walker, we will need contact information on the company that ran the Ferris wheel."

"I can get that for you."

"Good. Now, what about the other passengers on the wheel at the time?"

"Well, they were let off of the wheel and scattered before I got there. We don't know who they were, except for Glory Lockhart and Tom Rankin."

"Did you put out any public notice for others who were riding on the wheel at the time to contact you?" Steele sounded incredulous.

Chief Walker cleared his throat. "No."

"So you have no known witnesses to the crime, except for Mrs. Lockhart and the Ferris wheel operator?" Steel pressed.

"What about your forensic data?" Sherman asked.

"Dr. Johnston would have that, what little there is."

Steele nodded and got to his feet. "We'll talk with you later, after we've interviewed Lockhart and

Johnston and have a look around the scene. Oh—one more thing. Where was Rankin staying while he was here? We'd like to see his room."

"He had a room at our local motel, the Pot 'o Gold. I've still got the room ribboned off. I'll call the motel and tell them to let you in."

"Good, that will be a big help. Will you be here later this afternoon?"

"Yes." Chief Walker handed the two the information his receptionist had gotten for them. With that, Steele and Sherman went to their car.

Once inside, Sherman turned to Steele. "Well, Bill, what do you think?"

"I think we've got our work cut out for us."

"To say the least. Let's catch the medical examiner first."

Dr. Johnston's office and lab were in the civic building down the street from the station. Steele and Sherman went directly there and introduced themselves.

"Dr. Johnston, I'm Bill Steele and this is my partner, Joe Sherman, up from the FBI office in Rutland. We'd like to talk with you about the Rankin killing." He handed over their badges.

"Of course, of course. What do you need to know?" Dr. Johnston smiled and handed the badges back.

"All you know."

Dr. Johnston nodded. "Well, Rankin was shot in the back, through the gondola seatback with a nine millimeter round that was pretty well spent by the time it reached him and lodged in his heart. I'd say death was almost instantaneous."

"Spent? How?" Steele asked.

"Probably by the steel seatback of the gondola, but it could also have been that the killer was shooting from a distance. Hard to say, exactly. But the bullet didn't have much energy when it entered him."

"We understand the angle was slightly downward?" Sherman asked.

"That's right."

"So the weapon was fired from an elevation."

"It would seem so, but the Ferris wheel was in a flat field and there were no buildings behind it or any elevations around it."

Steele frowned.

"I think it was fired from another gondola that was above Rankin's as the wheel made its circuit," said Dr. Johnston.

"Interesting idea," Steele said. "And where's the bullet now?"

"I gave it to Chief Walker. And there's one other thing."

"Yes?"

"Although the bullet was the primary cause of death, Mr. Rankin's body was loaded with myristicin."

"Myristicin?" Steele asked.

"It's the poison contained in nutmeg and makes it so lethal in large quantities. I think someone was trying to poison Mr. Rankin but perhaps decided a bullet would be quicker. Only a guess, you understand."

"I understand." Steele nodded. "That's certainly an added twist to our story. Well, thank you very much, Dr. Johnston. If you think of anything else, call us at the main number on this card. Where is Mrs. Lockhart's antique shop?"

"Just down on Main. Not far. Easy walk." Dr. Johnston pointed.

Steele looked at Sherman, "I think I'd rather see the scene first. Then we can interview Mrs. Lockhart."

The area where the Ferris wheel had been was at the rear of the county fairgrounds. Chief Walker had been right, it was flat as could be and no elevations, natural or man-made, behind it for as far as the eye could see. Police tape still encircled the area. Taking note, Sherman said, "That's a blessing. It'll circumscribe our search for the shell casing. I'll call home and get them to send a detail up right away."

"Good idea, but don't hold your breath for them finding anything of value." Steele pointed at the trampled ground where the Ferris wheel had stood. A quick walk around confirmed the futility of the situation, and the gathering clouds in the western sky meant that what little evidence might have been gleaned from the myriad of impressions in the dusty soil would soon be washed away. With a shrug, Steele accepted the lost opportunity and said, "Let's go see what Rankin's room can tell us."

The Pot 'o Gold was a five-minute ride to the opposite end of town from the fair grounds. The proprietor, Mr. Potter, was a short round man whose abdomen preceded him.

On seeing Steele and Sherman's badges, he waved them further into the lobby. "Gentlemen, gentlemen. Welcome to the Pot 'o Gold at Rainbow's End. It's not very often that we have members of our federal government visiting us. Pretty important case, is it? The victim must have been pretty important, eh? Eh? Otherwise you guys wouldn't be wasting your time here in our little out-of-the-way village. Eh? Eh?"

"We'd like to see the room Mr. Rankin occupied, please," said Steele.

"Of course, of course," said Mr. Potter, scuttling around from behind the counter. "Right this way."

The room was a typical two-star motel room. Comfortable, small, a bit threadbare. Mr. Potter tried to stay in the room with Steele and Sherman, but Sherman quickly maneuvered him to the door and out, closing it quietly in his face as he protested that perhaps he could help them.

Sherman looked at Steele. "Shouldn't take more than an hour for the whole village to know we're here."

"Oh, I figured that happened about five minutes after we left Walker. The blessings of a small town." Steele smiled. "Well, let's get to it."

The two systematically took the room and its contents apart, but found nothing to help them better understand Rankin's death.

"There's just not much here, Bill," Sherman said with a sigh.

"It would seem. . . .Wait! Look in the Bible!"

Sherman opened the desk drawer and took out the Gideon Bible. He flipped through the pages. Sure enough in the middle of the book of Romans, he found a slip of paper with what appeared to be gibberish written on it. It read: PIFYIT OIAZHKHMPP AAZXUOS FEOWL VEPYUZ WPRNG TGADSVVV NXEPN QVWCP ZRSVQT XSPNBNKM ALI MSK. "Doesn't make any sense," he observed and handed the sheet to Steele, who looked at it and shook his head.

"Tom was always dabbling with encryption—but wait—was there anything else on the page?"

Sherman nodded at the slip of paper in Steele's hands. "You're seeing all there is."

"No, I mean on the page in the Bible where it was stuck."

Sherman looked. "Yes, there's a phrase underlined. *Commend unto thee.*"

"That's it! That's the key!" Steele fairly shouted.

"The key? The key to what?"

"To Tom's encryption. He's left us a coded message," Steele said.

"But what's the code? There are millions of codes, all the way from simple frequency counts to the German Enigma. How do we know which one he's using?"

"Let's think for a moment. Tom was always reading, right?"

"I know. I couldn't even get him to put his books down long enough to sit in on our weekly poker game."

"I know! I know what it was." Steele closed his eyes, remembering. "He was reading about the Confederates in the Civil War. And the Rebels had only a limited number of codes and only one used a key phrase for translation."

"But which one?"

"The Vicksburg Square. Get some paper and we'll see if we can decode his message."

And so for the next hour the two agents pored over Tom's message and a 26 by 26 letter alphabetic matrix.

At last, Steele sat back, satisfaction written across his face. "Now we've gotten somewhere!" He handed Sherman the sheet with the decoded message on it. It read: *Nutmeg Long trail N. Monthly Slade Rankin Scott Ashford black widow Snotch Lockhart the key*

"Let's go see Mrs. Lockhart." Steele stood and led the way.

After a brief walk, the pair were standing in front of Glory's shop. The jangle of the hanging string of bells on the door announced their entrance.

Lilly greeted them with a friendly smile. "Looking for anything special?"

"Are you Mrs. Lockhart?" Steele queried.

"Me? Oh, no." Lilly turned toward the back shop. "Glory!" she bellowed. "Two gentlemen to see you."

Glory came through the door on the back wall of the shop? "Yes?"

"Mrs. Lockhart?" Steele stepped forward holding out his FBI badge. "My name's Bill Steele and this is my partner, Joe Sherman. May we have a word with you?"

Taken aback, Glory managed a smile. "Of course, come to my office." She led the two into the small room that served as office and rest area for the shop. "How may I help you?"

"Mrs. Lockhart, we're investigating the apparent murder of Thomas Rankin and, if you don't mind, we would like to hear your version of what happened that night."

Shocked, Glory hesitated momentarily and then told Steele and Sherman how her friends had arranged a blind date for her and Tom, how they had met at the Ferris wheel, and then went to the target shooting booth, where Tom won her a large teddy bear. Then they got on the Ferris wheel and when it was their turn to get off, Tom was slumped in the gondola beside her and the teddy, dead.

"And we were told that you did not know Tom Rankin before that night. Is that correct?" asked Sherman.

Glory hesitated a moment. "Yes, that's right. Never saw him before."

"Are you sure?" Steele pressed.

Glory laughed nervously, "Oh, yes, quite sure. Tom was a blind date."

"All right, Mrs. Lockhart. That will be all for now. If we think of anything else, we will contact you. And thank you for your time."

Steele and Sherman returned to their car.

"She's lying through her teeth," said Steele, buckling his seatbelt.

"What makes you say that?" asked Sherman.

"Remember, Joe, this is a very small town. The kids from around here all go to one central school—and since Tom was from another small town in this area, I'll wager you both he and Mrs. Lockhart went to the same school. I'd be willing to be she knew him, or at least *of* him."

"Why would she lie to us?"

"Good question. Let's get back to Walker and fill him in a bit. But let's keep the message Tom left us to ourselves for now, shall we?"

"You're the boss."

They headed back to the police station.

"Have a good look around?" Chief Walker asked as he ushered them again into his office.

"Very informative," said Steele. "You're certainly right. There're no elevations around the fairgrounds. Hard to account for the angle of the path of the bullet unless Dr. Johnston's theory is correct. I do have one question. Are you sure Mrs. Lockhart had never met Tom Rankin before their blind date?"

"That's what she maintains. Why?"

"Didn't they both attend the same central school north of Rainbow's End?"

"I'm not sure. We can check that easily enough," said the chief.

"Check that for us, will you, and let us know what you find out."

"Gladly. Now I have a question for you."

"Yes?"

"Does the Bureau have some interest in this case beyond the fact that Tom Rankin had been an agent?"

Steele paused. "Well, as I said it's both professional and personal. Tom was a fellow agent and friend. The rest of it is that the Bureau sent him up here to gather information. You see, we're in the midst of an investigation into smuggling."

"Smuggling? Here in Vermont? In Rainbow's End?"

"Oh, yes. Vermont has long been a hotbed of smuggling. Dates back to the Revolution and has continued, on and off, ever since. There was one particularly active period back during the Civil War. Confederates used the Long Trail through the mountains—runs all the way from Sherburne to the Canadian border—to run contraband and cash for their war efforts. There are even a series of caves along the trail where contraband has been hidden over the years. You should read your local history."

"Maybe I should," said Chief Walker, rubbing his chin thoughtfully. "Tell me more."

Steele nodded. "Well, every once in a while smugglers reactivate the trail and use the caves. Now is one of those times, and we sent Tom Rankin here to see if he could learn anything."

"And did he?"

"We think so. That's probably why he was murdered," said Sherman.

"But what are they smuggling?" asked Chief Walker.

"We think the main thing is nutmeg," Steele answered.

"*Nutmeg*? You eat that!"

"In very small quantities, I hope." Steele smiled. "You see, even in doses as small as a teaspoon or two it is a rather powerful hallucinogenic. It's starting to get a play in some of the East Coast cities and the drug dealers need increasing quantities to support their operations. Tom's death has only served to confirm the magnitude of the problem in Vermont right now. You can understand our involvement."

"I certainly can. Are you aware that there's a restaurant north of here in Clairville called the Nutmeg's?"

"Interesting. Maybe we'll stop there before we go back to Rutland. In the meantime, let us know if anything turns up of interest and if I were you, I'd keep an eye on Mrs. Lockhart. She's not telling us all she knows about Tom's shooting.

Chapter 11
by David Selcer

Glory was beginning to lose her self-confidence. Learning that her old high school beau Slade was Tom's brother had been disconcerting to be sure, but not enough to really rattle her. Nor was her visit with Connie just yesterday at Nutmeg's in Clairville, or finding Slade in the poor condition he was in.

Looking back thirty-six years, she realized that even back then she had known him to be a nut—a fun one, but a nut, nonetheless.

Now, however, two FBI agents had shown up to question her. She knew that for them to be involved, there had to be some federal question concerning Tom, perhaps a crime crossing state lines, or the violation of some federal law or the Constitution, and that was scaring her a lot. On top of that, she knew that she knew too much.

All she had told Steele and Sherman was that she had been on a blind date with Tom, that they had met at the Ferris wheel, then gone to the shooting game and back to the Ferris wheel for a ride—that when she and Tom had gone up in the Ferris wheel, they were having a good time, but when they came down as the ride ended, he was dead.

She'd told Chief Walker more than that, but not the FBI. Was she going to be in trouble now? Why hadn't she just taken Tyler's advice and simply stayed out of the whole thing other than to tell the story of what had happened on the wheel? She could have just left it at that.

Ron had always said that when he interrogated a person who had something to hide, they would usually just answer the questions and stop, never volunteering anything extra. Their lawyer son, Cameron, had once told her that he advised his clients, when he was examining them in court, to tell the whole truth, explaining everything, but that when the opposing lawyer was cross-examining them, they should simply give a short answer to the question and stop at that.

Glory wondered whether she a suspect. Were there going to be "sides" concerning her story? Was she going to need to be coached on how to handle herself on the stand?

Perhaps that was why, when Agent Steele had said the FBI would like to hear her version of what had happened the night Tom died, she had given such a short answer. She'd omitted the part about the sudden look of fear on Tom's face as he glanced sideways looking toward the crowd on the ground, not to mention what he'd said to her. She'd gone over his words again and again in her mind. *Oh, god. I didn't realize the hole I've dug for myself until just now.* And he had been shaking. But most importantly, Glory hadn't told the FBI that just before he died, Tom had sputtered out an admission that, contrary to what he'd previously told her, he *had* known her husband—*but it's not what you think*, he'd said.

What had he thought she was thinking?

Now it could be claimed that there were inconsistencies in her story, things she might later have to explain. Disparities and omissions always led to credibility questions in federal cases, whereas when just the local chief was investigating, she could be assured any answers she gave would receive a friendly reception. Chief Walker knew her—had known Don. But to the FBI, she was nobody special.

She began worrying about all the other things she might have done wrong—things she should've been careful to tell Chief Walker. Like how on the night she left the scene of Tom's death, she'd stepped on something she'd taken to be a child's kaleidoscope at the time. Of course, later she'd realized she had been mistaken. It had been a rifle scope. She knew this because somewhere deep down, she still remembered watching Slade Rankin use similar scopes at high school shooting contests, where he had been considered quite the marksman.

Where else had she slipped up? Perhaps her biggest mistake was not sitting down at her computer and googling Tom Rankin to find out who and what he really was, either before she met him or after he died. Instead, she had simply relied on Max and Connie to vouch for his bona-fides because they were such good friends of hers. At least she thought they were. Yet Max had exploded at her over the terror Connie had experienced on their visits to Slade Rankin and Scott Ashford during their recent sojourn to Northern Vermont together. Max was so angry with Glory he wasn't going to allow Connie to go anywhere with her again. How would that look to others? Max was angry, but Connie wasn't. She had just been shaken up after meeting Slade.

Glory ran over all of these things in her mind after the agents had gone on their way. She numbly arranged and rearranged a display of antique toys. Then she suddenly remembered her promise to Connie to ask Lilly whether she knew if *Mary A* from the tree trunk across the river from Scott Ashford's acreage was any relation to Ashford himself—or more specifically, whether she was his sister. On one hand, Glory knew she shouldn't delve any further into the matter by asking more questions, but on the other, she just couldn't stop at this point. She had to find out if Tom's former fiancée, Mary A, was any relation to the man whose deed Tom had apparently sent her.

She was beginning to have doubts that it was actually Tom who had sent her the deed, along with the check for ten thousand dollars payable to Ashford and the note instructing her to deliver these items to him on pain of a threat against someone close to her. She had never seen Tom's handwriting, so maybe he hadn't written the note at all. Thus, there was no real evidence that established any connection between Tom and Ashford, and the papers Glory had received could have been sent by someone *posing* as Tom. On the other hand, if Mary A was an Ashford, that would certainly lay open the question as to whether a connection between Ashford and Tom existed.

Lilly's family was one of the oldest in Rainbow's End, as was Ashford's. Lilly herself might not know about the old connections between the Ashfords and Tom, but someone in Lilly's family would probably have an inkling. Lilly was still working in the front of the store, and no customers were present, so Glory felt the time was right to approach her about this. She asked her to come to the backroom.

"Lilly, I'm looking into some questions I have about that deed and check I received Sunday. Remember the manilla envelope?"

"Of course. How could I forget?"

"Well, this is a very sensitive matter, and I think you may be able to help me."

"Sure, Glory. I'll do anything I can to help."

"I need some information but I can't tell you why. In fact, I'm going to have to ask you not to even hint to anyone that I'm asking this, because I'm afraid of the threat in that note."

"I don't blame you! Of course I'll keep this private. What is it you want to know?"

"Okay." Glory let out a nervous sigh. "Well, here's my question. You or someone in your family might know the answer, since yours is one of the oldest families in town. Does Scott Ashford have a sister named Mary?"

Lilly thought for a moment. "The only sister I know of is in a mental institution. I don't know her name, but I'll check to see if anyone in my family does. The Ashfords have always been a strange bunch as far as I know, and they keep everything about themselves pretty close to the vest, so to speak." Lilly laid a hand on Glory's shoulder. "Don't worry. I'll find out."

Chapter 12
by Zaida Alfaro

Glory was not known to be a patient person. But after the conversation she'd had with Lilly, she had no choice. She'd have to wait until Lilly could dig up any information regarding the Ashford family history. So Glory decided to rearrange her storage room and re-index all the items she'd received over the last couple of years. The storage room was Glory's favorite part of her antique shop. Here she was surrounded by history. She had a rolling stepladder that would take her to the era she wanted to get lost in. Organizing the pieces always put Glory at ease. She liked to imagine the stories they had to tell.

She delicately picked up a miniature sculpture of a horse standing on its hind legs. The sculpture was a faded gray color, and the texture felt like cement. The horse's facial expression was strong, as if it were ready to go to war—but without its owner. She slowly stroked the mane of the horse. "What happened to your owner?" Glory whispered to the statue. She flipped it over and found engraved on its base the year 1924. Glory recalled the young college woman who'd sold her the piece. She'd told Glory that her grandfather had left her the statue, but she figured someone else would enjoy its history more than she would—and that she needed the extra money.

Glory's thoughts shifted to the encounter she'd had with Slade. She had the distinct impression she was missing a clue. What kind of message was Slade trying to give her when he'd used the phrase, *You must lie down where all the ladders start. In the foul rag and bone of the heart*? She felt as though he'd been holding back. Was it because Connie and the unidentified woman were there? At first, it had appeared that Slade was taken aback by Connie's presence—or maybe Glory had just imagined that hint of momentary surprise.

Slade had always been odd, but he'd always had an artistic mind. Glory supposed that was what attracted her to him in high school. Slade was a drifter—mentally speaking—and Glory was his constant element. But she didn't understand that back then.

She moved the stepladder, took a few steps up, and placed the horse where it belonged, next to a deluxe edition of the *Complete Works of William Shakespeare*. Glory loved the smell of old books. It was a distinguished scent that, for Glory, new books lacked.

"I'm heading out to lunch, unless you need help in here," Lilly said, peeking into the storage room door.

"No, I'm good. This is therapeutic for me," Glory said with a chuckle, coming down the stepladder.

"I'm going to meet my cousin Sharon for lunch to see if I can get any information from her."

"Good. But remember to be very discreet. I wasn't even supposed to get you involved. I'm already in a big heap of trouble for even meeting up with Slade and putting Connie in danger."

"Don't worry. I'm going to tell Sharon that we received a piece of art, and that I think it's connected to the Ashford family, and see where it goes from there," Lilly said.

"Thank you for doing this. I do appreciate it," Glory said with a smile.

"Anything to help a friend out. I'll see you in about an hour, hopefully with some good news."

"Oh, Lilly!"

Lilly turned.

"Can you please hang the 'Out to lunch,' sign and lock the front door? I'm not done in here yet."

"Sure. See you later."

Glory was about to move the stepladder when a thought occurred to her. "You must lie down where all the ladders start. In the foul rag and bone of the heart." This time, Glory said it out loud, staring at her wooden stepladder. She traced the railing of the ladder with her eyes. She was standing at the end—or maybe it was the beginning of where the step ladder started. "I may be onto something," she whispered.

Glory's late husband, Ron, had always complimented her on how intelligent she was when it came to solving puzzles, especially Sudoku. Glory never understood why he would stress himself out with puzzles, but Ron would tell her that it was a way for him to challenge his mind. The thought of her late husband put a smile on Glory's face.

"Focus," Glory said out loud. She repeated the lines of poetry once more and looked up at her bookcase. She pushed the step ladder to the other end of the bookcase, and started climbing the ladder step by step, analyzing all the contents that were on the wooden shelves as she went. Glory had no idea what she was looking for. She felt silly even thinking that a clue was hidden amongst her treasures.

"What am I doing?" she muttered. She laughed at herself and decided to continue organizing, reminding herself that she had to remain calm and patient until Lilly returned—hopefully, with some information.

Glory maneuvered the ladder back to the other end of the bookcase, climbed up a few steps, and adjusted the statue of the horse one last time, admiring the craftsmanship while mumbling, "in the foul rag and bone of the heart." Then something clicked in her mind. It was something that she'd previously read, she was sure of it.

Her attention shifted from the statue to the book next to it. She carefully slid the *Complete Works of William Shakespeare* off the shelf and carried it back down the stepladder to her desk. She pulled out her antique chair and seated herself. She was facing the entrance of the storage room. She'd already made sure that the door was properly closed. Glory stared at the book for a moment, thinking, then clicked on her Victorian desk lamp.

She knew the contents of this book very well—she'd read it in spare moments here and there for ages. She opened the cover and breathed in the book's familiar aroma, then scrolled through the table of contents with her index finger, stopping at the section titled, "The Words on William Shakespeare's Tombstone." Glory quickly flipped to that chapter, and there, tucked deep between the pages, was a thin, faded white envelope addressed to her. With trembling fingers, she lifted the envelope out of the book. Her gaze shifted to the page the book was opened to. She read through the words on Shakespeare's tombstone. One sentence caught her attention. *And cursed be he that moves my bones.*

Her gaze returned to the envelope, a single tear trickling down her warm cheek. She knew the handwriting as well as she knew her own. On anniversary greeting cards, on Valentines, and on every birthday card, Ron would write, "I will love you always, my sweet Glory."

Glory clutched the envelope as if she were hugging her late husband. There was a whirlwind of emotions, now mixed with many new questions that she didn't have the answers to. Had Ron known all of this would come to pass? Had he indirectly been involved in

Tom's death? How could he have known that she would find this letter? Did he know Slade? There was only one way to find out.

Glory turned the envelope over, grabbed the letter opener from her penholder, and carefully slid it under the flap, breaking the seal. She pulled out a single sheet of light purple paper. Her favorite color. She smiled thinking that Ron had remembered that minor detail. She unfolded the letter. It was dated one week prior to Ron's death. She put a hand over her mouth and closed her eyes. Glory knew Ron would want her to be strong, so she inhaled, opened her eyes, gently wiped away her tears, and started reading the letter to herself.

My sweet Glory. If you are reading this letter, unfortunately, it means that things did not turn out as I had planned. On a side note, if you are reading this letter, then I am extremely impressed. As I told you many times before, I have always been so awe-struck by your puzzle solving abilities but I had to hide this where I knew only you could possibly find it.

Glory stopped reading, not sure she could continue. A rush of memories came back to her, and the sorrow she was feeling now felt the same as the sorrow she'd experienced at Ron's funeral. But she knew this was the key to figuring out what was going on. She couldn't think of herself now—she had to finish what she'd started. Glory turned back to Ron's letter.

I'm sure you're very confused by the complexity of the situation at hand, so I will explain this to you as simply as I possibly can. Tom Rankin, a federal agent, came to me about two years ago. His brother Slade Rankin was somehow involved in a drug case he was investigating. I remembered you telling me you had dated him in high school. I'll come clean now—when I was casually and randomly asking you questions about your high school sweetheart, I was really trying to get a feel about what kind of a person I was dealing with. I was hoping you wouldn't catch on.

Glory looked up from the letter and remembered the random questions Ron had asked her back then. He would joke around, and tell her that he wanted to make sure there was no comparison between him and her high school sweetheart—but Ron had never been the jealous type. Now, it made sense to Glory. She continued reading the letter.

Tom's investigation had led him to a drug ring that was using certain trails through our town to smuggle unidentified drugs. Tom found out that his brother was somehow involved. I was to meet with Tom and talk about a plan that would benefit both our local police department and the bureau, without putting Slade in jeopardy. Tom was trying to minimize the punishment Slade would receive for collaborating with a set of unidentified drug dealers. He was holding off on telling the FBI. But when the day of our meeting came, Tom never showed up.

Glory could not believe what she was reading.

"Glory, did you hear me?" Lilly had returned and was addressing her from the doorway.

Glory snapped the Shakespeare book shut with the letter inside. "No, I'm sorry, I zoned out."

"You really love that book. I'm sure you have all the sonnets memorized by now," Lilly said with a grin. "Anyway, no luck with Sharon, but she's going to put in a call to her friend, who's an Ashford. Hopefully, I can set up a lunch with him sooner rather than later. Oh, and she's finally dating someone! It's about time. That sweet girl needs a good man in her life."

"Thank you," was all Glory could manage to say.

"I'll be out by the register." Lilly went back into the showroom, closing the door behind her.

Glory opened the book and took out the letter, then carefully folded it. Now was not the time to read it, she realized, as she might need to decipher more puzzles within the letter. She had a store to run, after all, and she couldn't act like something was wrong, not until she figured this out for herself.

Glory placed the letter back into the envelope and turned it over. She slowly traced her name on the front with her fingers. "Oh Ron, what did you get us into?" she whispered.

She tucked the envelope into her purse, put her purse in the desk drawer, and locked it. She slowly stood up and stretched. As much as she wanted to read the remainder of the letter, she knew she'd have to do it with time and caution. Just as she was stepping out of the storage room, she ran into Connie.

"Hi. I hope you don't mind. Lilly told me you were back here."

"Hi. Gosh, I'm so happy to see you." Glory paused. "Is Max still livid with me about our little adventure?"

"I'm sorry about all that. It's just—are you okay? You look flushed."

"Oh, yes. I was just in there a bit too long, I guess." Glory closed the storge room door and led Connie into the store.

Connie looked around nervously. "Can we meet tonight at Larry's Diner?" she whispered.

Glory tilted her head and gently looked at her friend. "Are you okay?"

"I just really need to speak to you about, well, about Tom." The door chime jingled, and Connie looked toward the entrance, startled. An older gentleman came in carrying a painting. Connie turned quickly back to Glory, "So, can you?"

"Yes, yes, of course. I can be there at seven."

"Perfect," Connie said. She grabbed Glory's left hand, "Don't worry; everything is going to turn out okay. I've got to go. See you at seven." She headed out of the store.

Glory stood there at a loss for a few seconds. She didn't know how to react to any of this. She mentally outlined the questions she needed answers to. What did Connie know? Should she tell Tyler about the letter from his father, or should she wait until she'd fully read it herself? Could she trust Agents Steele and Sherman? Glory's mind was like a never-ending roller-coaster ride these days.

"Glory, can you check out this piece for me?" Lilly said from the register.

She fixed her hair and straightened out her shirt, and exhaled. "I'll be right there."

Chapter 13
by Karen Shughart

Glory worked the rest of the day feeling anxious about Ron's letter and unsettled about Connie's invitation to dinner. Something wasn't right; she just couldn't put her finger on it.

She had just enough time after closing the shop to go home, freshen up and change her clothes. Larry's Diner was a casual place, so she threw on a pair of jeans and a light sweater and slipped into sandals before heading out. *Might as well be comfortable,* she thought.

The diner was an odd choice to meet for a discussion about Tom Rankin. It was bright and noisy with servers bellowing out orders to short order cooks, and lots of happy, boisterous patrons. Glory desperately wanted a glass of wine to calm her nerves, but the diner didn't serve alcohol. A drink would have to wait.

Connie was waiting for her at the entrance. "I expect you're wondering why I asked you to meet me here to talk about Tom," she said, reading Glory's thoughts. "I chose it because it's safe and very public. I believe I know who was following us in the blue car the other day, and he won't harm us here."

Glory just shook her head. *This is getting weirder and weirder.* Now one of her closest friends, someone she had trusted, seemed to be implying knowledge of Tom and what had happened to him.

The friends were able to find a cozy booth in a corner, away from the door. After ordering glasses of iced tea, they perused their menus, but Glory really wasn't hungry. She ordered a small garden salad with grilled chicken, dressing on the side; her friend's appetite didn't seem much diminished. Connie ordered a cheeseburger, large fries, and fried pickles.

"Connie, you don't seem stressed out, but my head's spinning: Tom's death, the deed and check, Ashford's possible involvement, that bizarre interaction with Slade and the woman in his restaurant, the spider graffiti, the blue car. I'm not sure I can take much more. Please tell me what you know about Tom Rankin. The suspense is killing me."

"Oh, Glory. I'm so sorry. I've kept things from you that I should have told you long ago. You had a right to know, but Max said I shouldn't muddy the waters, that it was better to keep you in the dark to protect you. I've been lying to you about why we fixed you up with Tom."

Impatient and beginning to feel a bit angry, Glory looked at her friend in amazement. "You deceived me? How could you? Can you even imagine what I've been through the past couple days? The past *year*? I lost my husband and witnessed the murder of a very attractive man whom I enjoyed being with. We even talked about having another date. But now—"

Just then the server delivered their meals, and, assured that they needed nothing more, he walked over to the next table to check on his customers there.

Connie gazed up at the ceiling for a moment as if to pray. "Max and Tom met in the service. Tom went on to join the FBI, and when he came to town this time, he asked us if we could arrange a date between you and him. He thought he might be able to learn something from you about his previous cases."

Glory frowned.

Connie continued, "Then when Tom was killed, and the FBI sent agents Steele and Sherman to town to investigate, they became convinced that you were involved in Tom's murder, but Max and I assured them of your innocence. I just felt you needed to be brought into the loop."

"Why didn't you just tell me when Tom first arrived? Why all the subterfuge?"

"I'm so sorry, Glory. I just couldn't tell you. It could have put your life and those of your children at risk. Tom thought that the less you knew, the better, and we promised him. Max wasn't angry with me the other day for going with you to meet with Scott and Slade; he was angry because he felt I hadn't done enough to persuade you to stay away."

This was more information than Glory could absorb, and she shook her head. "I want a glass of wine. Or maybe a sleeping pill. I want to go to sleep and wake up to discover this has all just been a very bad dream...a nightmare."

Connie put her hand over Glory's. She told Glory that whenever Tom came to town to visit, it typically was because of a case he was working on. This time it had been because he had evidence that Ron had been killed because the driver and passenger of a car he'd stopped—a blue car—had been smuggling hundreds of pounds of myristicin, an illegal drug, toward the Canadian border. When Ron had asked them to step out of the car, one of them shot him, and the pair drove away.

"How do I fit into this, Connie? Why did you fix me up with Tom?"

"We thought the idea of a blind date was a good cover. Tom hoped he'd be able to learn from you more about the day Ron was killed, but it was never his intention to become involved with you, at least not romantically. We didn't think there would be any chemistry and after a date or two you'd realize it, and that would be that. And you'd stay safe."

"Well, that explains why he was asking me so many questions," Glory said, bursting into tears. "Connie, how could you? Do you know how vulnerable I am? I thought he was so attractive, and he seemed to like me, and now you're telling me he—all of you—were using me?" Then she paused. "Oh, my."

"What?"

"There *was* chemistry between us. He acted surprised when we first met and again after I told him Ron had been my husband. Of course, he was dissembling, but then later he said, '*I didn't realize the hole I've dug for myself until just now.*' He was shaking. We definitely felt attracted to each other, I'm certain of it, and it must have shocked him, especially since that wasn't part of his original plan."

"You're right, Glory. You must have been distracted by something and didn't notice, but just before he was shot, Tom texted Max and me. He said, 'She's fabulous, now what do I do?' Liking you complicated the situation. You see, Tom wasn't single. It's true he had a fiancée, and her name was Mary Ashford, but they didn't break up. He married her, but to protect her, he never told her about what he was doing with the FBI."

Connie continued, "He had busted a drug ring and confiscated the drugs. During the bust, one of the suspects was shot and killed; a couple of them got away. When Tom got home that night he found Mary unconscious, lying in a pool of blood. She'd been shot in the spine and head, and there was a note beside her with the word *REVENGE* on it. But Mary didn't die. She survived, but as a quadriplegic with extensive brain damage. She now resides in a nursing home.

"Tom blamed himself for what happened to her and, as a devoted husband, he visited her often. He may have wanted the relationship with you to go further but didn't know how to handle it. He and Mary had been happy before she'd been shot, and he vowed to take care of her for the rest of her life."

Glory pulled a tissue out of her purse and blew her nose. "Lilly told me Scott Ashford has a sister who's in a mental institution, but that's not true, is it? It's Mary, Tom's wife, living in the nursing home."

Connie nodded.

"How sad. But where does Slade fit into the picture? As you saw, he's a mess. What happened to him?"

"Tom said he thinks he got hooked on drugs, probably this myristicin he was smuggling. It was too tempting for someone with his personality to not sample the goods. The drug works slowly, so it took a while to damage his brain, but he's insane, his mind is gone. I'm not sure why he called you; maybe he was remembering your past relationship. Maybe he really wanted to warn you. He sees ghosts and goblins. The woman at the top of the steps is Slade and Tom's sister, Heather. She came to take care of him, but he's gotten worse, so she was getting ready to commit him to an institution."

Glory looked at her friend and realized that she would never view her in the same way again. The friendship, at least what it had been, was in the past, but she also realized there was more Connie wasn't telling her.

"I don't know if I can take any more bad news, Connie, but I think you're holding out on me. I sense it, and I'm very good at parsing details from people. Are Tyler and Chief Walker involved? Please tell me they aren't."

Connie shook her head. "No, Tyler and the chief know nothing, other than the few bits of information agents Steele and Sherman have shared with them. But there's one more thing. Although he wasn't in the blue car when Ron was killed, Tom was convinced that Slade had something to do with his death."

It was too much, way too much information for Glory to process. If Slade was involved with Ron's death, did it have anything to do with her aborted teenage romance with him? Had he been jealous of Ron, or did it have something to do with the drugs?

Scott Ashford must have been furious at Tom and blamed him for what had happened to his sister. Was he involved with Tom's murder? Was any of this connected to the murder of Scott's wife, Elise? Who was in the blue car that had been following them? Glory didn't ask and wasn't even sure Connie would tell her if she knew. Glory believed the agents were working on those angles, and she had enough information for now.

She wanted to go home, drink wine, and go to sleep. She pulled out her wallet, dropped cash on the table and without saying another word to her friend, left the diner. For now, Connie was *persona non grata* as far as Glory was concerned. Cameron was the only person she felt she could confide in at the moment, and, besides, he'd probably met Tom when he was a boy. Unfortunately, that conversation would have to wait.

Safe inside her home, Glory guzzled a glass of pinot grigio, took a hot bath, then pulled on a nightgown and collapsed onto her bed, falling into a fitful sleep. She awoke several hours later with a gasp and looked at the clock. It was 3:00 a.m. She had been dreaming of Ludwig Bemelmans' picture book, *Madeline*—a story she'd read aloud to her kids countless times. A couple of the sentences kept playing over and over in her head. "In an old house in Paris that was covered in vines....

In the middle of the night Miss Clavel turned on the light and said, 'Something is not right.'"

Something is not right, something is not right, she thought. *Why do I keep hearing that sentence, and why an old house in Paris? What does the book have to do with Tom's murder, if anything?* That was it. She realized something was off about this investigation. They were looking at it wrong, and the clues for righting it, she thought, might be hidden in the text of *Madeline.* At least her subconscious mind seemed to think so.

Throwing on an old, faded blue quilted robe, Glory went downstairs to the library, which was across the hall from the living room in the ancient house, and pulled the book off a shelf. Her children had loved the timeless story about the young girl in Paris, and it still delighted her grandchildren.

She started reading. Then it hit her. There was a woman by the name of Clavel—Nancy Clavel—at a party she'd attended with Ron a couple years ago. It had been Christmastime, and they'd been invited to the party by the mayor and his wife, whose family owned an estate in Paris, New Hampshire, just over the border from Rainbow's End.

She remembered that at the end of a long, narrow lane surrounded by woods stood a gatehouse. After Ron had given the security guard their names, she'd opened an iron gate. In front of them was a large stone house, covered with vines, that faced a circular driveway ringed with luminaria. They'd pulled into the driveway, and a valet had opened the car door for Glory and then walked around to the driver's seat, taking Ron's keys. Then she and Ron had entered the stately manse, beautifully decorated for the season with fresh greens and berries, lots of candles and fires roaring in fireplaces in each room. A string quartet played in the spacious living room.

They had wandered together for a while, then parted ways to mingle, as was their habit at social gatherings. After she'd had enough superficial chitchat with other guests, Glory grabbed a glass of champagne and decided to look for Ron. She found him standing in a circle with the mayor, two other men, and two very attractive young women. She started toward the group, but then stopped. The conversation looked serious, and she instinctively felt she wouldn't be welcomed if she interrupted, so she wandered away—but not before she noticed one of the men glancing at her.

A couple hours later, on their way back to Rainbow's End, Glory asked Ron about the incident. "I saw you speaking to a small group tonight. Who were they?"

Ron was evasive. "Oh, the mayor wanted me to meet some friends of his, nothing important."

"But *who* were they, Ron? Why won't you tell me?"

Ron glanced at his wife and sighed. "Nobody special. Truly. You certainly could have joined us. We were just making small talk."

Glory remembered that she'd wanted to argue with Ron, but she knew when to hold them and when to fold them so she didn't press for more information. Still, she didn't believe him. The two of them were quiet during the remainder of the trip, and shortly after they arrived home they went to bed. Ron had laid his suit jacket on a chair in their bedroom, and the next morning, when she picked it up to hang it in the closet, a business card had fallen out. It had an FBI insignia and a photo of one of the women he'd been speaking to at the party. Her name was Nancy Clavel, and she was head of a drug task force in New England.

Putting the card back into the pocket, Glory had hung up the coat. Ron had been killed shortly after that, and she hadn't yet been able to bring herself to get rid of his belongings.

Now she went into the closet and found the jacket. The card was still in the pocket. *I might need this*, she thought, as she pulled it out and placed it in a dresser drawer. The woman in the photo looked vaguely familiar, but not just because of the party. No, Glory had seen her recently.

And then she remembered something else. The other woman at that party had jet black hair and looked like a teenager. She was wearing a sleeveless black velvet mini dress, and tattooed on her left arm was a spider—a black widow spider. Just like the graffiti spider that had been painted onto Glory's building. With a flash, it hit her. She was the same woman as the gum-chewing ticket taker at the fair. Glory was sure of that. And she was positive she'd seen what she thought was a kaleidoscope, maybe a rifle scope, in that booth with her. As she thought back to the Christmas party, the memories grew sharper, and Glory remembered something else. Tom Rankin had been one of the other two men in the group that night. He'd been the one who had glanced at her! His shock when he met her at the fair was probably because he'd recognized her from the party.

By now Glory was wide awake. She was too agitated to go back to sleep and decided to make herself a cup of tea to calm her nerves.

Several hours later, showered and dressed, she drank a second cup of tea, quickly ate a toasted bagel, and then got into her car to drive to the Rainbow's End Community Library, where she spent several hours perusing digital newspaper files, dating back to just before Ron was killed. She finally found what she'd been looking for, an article about a young woman who'd been arrested for running a drug ring. The charges hadn't stuck, and she'd been released. Her name was an odd one. Glory should have remembered. Mala. Mala DeTritus. There was a picture of her grinning defiantly at the camera. She had jet-black hair and looked like a teenager. She wore a sleeveless blouse, and a huge black widow spider was tattooed on her left arm.

She was the woman at the Christmas party *and* the fair. But what would a drug runner be doing at that party? Or the fair? Glory was positive there was a connection between this woman and Ron's and Tom's deaths, and she aimed to find out what it was.

Slade had warned her about a clown and a man smoking at the fair, and he'd mentioned the stuffed bear. How could he have known about those things unless he'd been there or knew someone who was? Maybe they were real clues, but it also could be possible Slade was putting up a smokescreen to lead the investigation down the wrong path. Maybe he wasn't quite as crazy as he appeared. Glory drove home from the library, pulled Nancy Clavel's business card out of her drawer, grabbed her cell phone, and placed the call. Something certainly was not right.

Chapter 14
by Lane Buckman

Glory was muttering to herself and kneading the life out of a ball of bread dough when Joey came tromping through the kitchen.

"Denial, anger, bargaining, depression, and acceptance." He answered the question she'd been asking herself, ticking off a finger for each one. "The stages of grief."

"Are you sure anger isn't in there twice?" She leaned against the one-armed hug he'd slung her into.

"I guess you could be angrily depressed? Is this about Tom Rankin?" He pushed off from her, coming to rest against the kitchen sink, looking back over his shoulder. Likely checking to see if there were any beaters that needed licking. He'd already seen the cake layers cooling on the rack.

"Funnily enough, he's the least of my worries right now."

Humming, Joey lurched forward and threw himself into a chair. He was her most active child, the baby of the buch, and every action, no matter how mundane, seemed to come with an exclamation point, but his eyes were soft and calm. "Want to talk about it?"

She did want to talk about it, but she didn't want to worry him. She wanted to talk to Ron, but Ron was dead, likely the victim of a case he was coming too close to solving.

"Thank you, sweetie," she said. "But I don't think so."

She picked up and slammed down the dough, pounding into it with her fists before lifting it to the light of the late afternoon sun shining in through the kitchen window. It wouldn't take much more abuse before she'd have beaten the yeast right out of it, so with a heavy sigh she shaped it back into a ball, dropped it in the bowl she'd prepared for it, and put it away to rise.

Her son's eyes never left her as she moved to the oven, pulling the door down just as the timer went off. There were two dozen muffins inside. Those would be packed up in baskets along with the cookies and banana loaves she'd spent the past few hours whipping up from scratch in a marathon of rage-baking meant to calm her nerves and help clear her mind. She couldn't say it had done much good, but at least there would be treats for the police and fire departments. Maybe even the library. The town services could benefit from her trouble if they hadn't already become part of it.

"What's going on, Mom?"

"It's nothing to worry you about, Joe," she said. What could she tell the boy that wouldn't upset him? There wasn't much she could tell herself that didn't set her teeth on edge with raw panic.

After hanging up from her conversation with Nancy Clavel, Glory had done the thing she'd considered and rejected a hundred times since Ron's death. She'd logged into the laptop he'd left sitting on his bedside table and had started to go through personal files— notes he kept for himself outside of office hours—and had felt fear and outrage mounting with every bit of information she'd gleaned from a folder called, "Nutmeg."

"I'm already worried," Joey said quietly.

Glory hesitated, wiping her hands on a dish towel, looking up to the gingerbread trim Ron had so carefully installed just the way she'd seen it done in an interior style magazine. What could she tell her youngest son? How could she water down the truth?

"I'm not stupid," she said, backtracking at the look on Joey's face. "I mean, I am naive, but I'm not stupid. I'm just angry because I've had some people treating me like I don't even know how to work a search engine. I run a business, for crying out loud! I deal with all kinds of different people every day of my life, not to mention people trying to pull the wool over my eyes— telling me that their great aunt Virginia's tea kettle once served King George or whatever. I may not be a detective, but that doesn't mean I'm not smart enough to know when someone's lying to me."

She felt her eyes filling as she thought about Connie, and she blew out a harsh breath against the anger. Something in the back of her mind wondered if she had enough flour left for scones.

Joey was on his feet and had dragged his mother into a bear hug before the first tear hit her cheek. "Aw, Mom! I'm sorry! Nobody should make you feel stupid. You're one of the smartest people I know. And," he leaned away a little to smile down at her as he said, "you raised four boys, and I don't think we've ever gotten away with lying to you. You're better at finding out the truth than...than...Sherlock Holmes! You're as good a detective as anyone else might be. Just with fewer gadgets."

He hugged her tight again and she let out a laugh as she struggled to pull herself together. While he patted her back he said, "I know it's serious, though. You usually stop at the banana bread. Muffins don't happen unless it's dire—like that time Chance drove into the speaker box at Sonic. And bread too? I haven't seen bread happen since Cam told you guys he was going to change his major to art history."

Glory barked, remembering Ron's fury over the amount of tuition money they had wasted on Cam's undergraduate work after his third time changing majors. She had baked enough that weekend to send him back to campus with food for his whole dormitory floor. Look at him now. Ron was so proud of his boys. He would have been so proud of Joey, who was doing his best to help his mother.

Having made her laugh, Joey released her and spun back toward his chair. "I'm not a kid, Mom. You can tell me stuff."

But something in the way he leaned forward, earnest elbows on his knees, made him look anything but grown. Still, the events of the past few days had clarified weak points in her alliances and, right that moment, she wasn't sure she wanted to extend her trust beyond the small circle of her family. She wasn't even sure she could trust Ned. She made a decision. If what she had discovered was right, this would involve them all. And if she was wrong? Well, she was going to need someone to bail her out of jail.

"Do me a little favor." She smiled at her son. "Call Chance and ask him to come home. I'm calling Cameron and Tyler. We all need to talk."

A few hours later, all of Glory's boys were sitting around the kitchen table in various stages of stuffed as they made short work of the baked goods while she talked. After catching them up on the misadventures of the past few days, spending a good amount of time on the conversation she'd last had with Connie, she came to her phone call with Nancy Clavel.

"She didn't quite laugh at me," Glory offered sheepishly, looking at Tyler through her lashes. "But she did explain that the FBI wouldn't share information with civilians. I guess I should have known that.

"She also explained that the FBI would never have put a civilian in a situation like the one Connie had described about—well, the date with Tom."

"So, I went into your father's computer—something I haven't done in our whole marriage."

"Because computers weren't invented yet," Chance said around a mouthful of bread, grunting as he took an elbow from Cameron.

"Well," Glory snorted at him, "since we've had computers in the house. I've never looked in his files. Today, I did."

Tyler held up a hand. "Mom, this sounds like official police business and I'm not sure—"

"I'm not either," Glory interrupted, plowing forward. "But I'm also not sure we can trust Ned anymore. Based on your father's notes and on a—hunch. It's a hunch. I have a strong suspicion that the drug ring the 'FBI' is looking into is run by Connie and Max themselves. I just have to prove it.

"Connie and Max want me to believe they were working with your father to bring down this ring, but I think they killed your father to keep him from proving they were the problem all along. And..." She hesitated.

"And what, Mom?" Chance asked, breathlessly.

"And I think I can prove it."

No one spoke for several minutes. Then, Glory realized they were all looking expectantly toward Tyler. For his part, he stared down at his hands, twirling his wedding band with the fingers of his right hand. When he looked up he was incredulous. "Slade Rankin? You dated Slade Rankin?"

Cameron hooted at him. "That's your takeaway? Mom tells you she thinks that her best friend is the mastermind of a drug ring that Dad was trying to take down, and that might very well be behind his death, and you're worried about who she dated in high school? You dated Sandy Carpenter! You've got no room to—"

"Sandy was a nice girl," Tyler yelped over his brother's next words. "She just… she got into some trouble."

"With drugs. Probably that Max and Connie and this Tom fellow sold her."

Glory cleared her throat.

"We're losing the plot, boys. I did date Slade Rankin, who was always good to me, if ultimately not the right man for me. I do think he's always kept an eye on me, though, and I do think he really meant for me to get something out of what he was saying the other day. I don't think it was all crazy talk. Furthermore, I think we can count him out as a suspect in your father's death. If Connie was leading me to him as the triggerman—"

"Listen to Mom talking like an episode of *CSI*," Joey teased.

Glory rolled her eyes. "If Connie was pointing me to Slade, that makes me think he's probably a liability for her. She was with me when he was talking about the clown and the bear."

Tyler looked skeptical but said, "I can help you with the bear. I'll check out the bear. And I can pull information on Mala DeTritus."

"That's got to be a fake name," Cameron said, laughing. "Bad debris? That's brilliant. Let me look into her."

Tyler had squared his shoulders. "Can I see Dad's laptop?"

Glory rose from the table, "Of course. I'll get it."

"If she looks like a teenager, maybe she's Chance's or my age?" Joey offered, still on the topic of Mala. "I'm going to go get my yearbooks."

Glory shook her head. "She's not from here. The article I saw said she was from New Jersey. And she wouldn't have been in a news report with a fake name."

"Then her parents have a weird sense of humor. Anyway, I'll look into her." Cameron cracked his knuckles. "Juicy!"

Joey wrinkled his nose. "But the spider thing. Hang on." He got up and left the table.

"I can ask about where they found the 'talent' for the carnival," Chance said, getting up. "I'm pretty sure my friend Clara was in on the planning. She works in the Parks and Rec department. She might know where the clowns came from—maybe even the company that supplied the carnies and ticket takers. Actually, I'll call her right now."

The boys started suggesting other areas of interest to investigate, with Tyler taking charge until Glory came back with the laptop and Joey came back with his last two yearbooks. Sure enough, there were those black widow spiders throughout, popping up on the upper arms and t-shirts of three students—and in one crowd shot from the homecoming football game, Glory swore she was looking at that spider on the blurry figure of Max. She sat back with a growl.

"All this time, I've thought your father's death was just a hazard of the job—a senseless act of violence."

"We all did," Tyler said. He paused a moment. "Mom? That letter you got that said one of your family was in danger? What if that meant you? And what if you were supposed to be so busy trying to protect one of us that you inadvertently exposed yourself?"

"I just don't see how that adds up."

"Me either, yet. But generally, when drug lords are tying up loose ends, they consider anyone left with a thread to pull on as a liability. Seems to me like you've got a whole lot of threads that Dad left behind."

"Well, I know one way to find out." Glory's eyes were blazing.

Chance slipped back in, sliding his phone into his pocket. "I told Clara I'm trying to find staff for the church carnival and asked if she could point me in the right direction. You're not going to believe this. Clara said the carnival staff came through an agency called Nutmeg, LLC. Guess who recommended that group? Nutmeg was full service and provided all the staff for the booths and ride crews, and even the walk-around talent."

Tyler tilted his head. "A carnival would be the perfect cover for a drug ring. You go from town to town with all kinds of crazy setups to carry around with you. You're crossing state lines without a glance. And, you have perfect access to young people who might be off wandering without supervision."

"Mom!" Joey cried. "I'll bet that bear is full of drugs! I'll bet that was a setup for Tom Rankin to move drugs with that bear! Or get you to move them. You were almost a drug mule! And...Mom! What if Slade Rankin was dressed like that clown and he shot his own brother to protect you?"

They all sat staring in the silence that hung from Joey's supposition. It was almost a perfect solution. Perfect enough for a TV script.

Glory shook her head. "If I hadn't seen a man shot dead in front of my eyes on a Ferris wheel, been handed a threat and a land deed, discovered my high school boyfriend was a drug-wasted ghost of a man, had my store graffitied, and learned that my best friend in the world might very well be the next Griselda Blanco all within the space of a few days, I would scoff at the very idea. However, since I have..."

Now that she was talking it out with her family, Glory was feeling a sense of relief and a burgeoning hopeful determination. Life had been a fog of confusion and worry since she'd gotten off that Ferris wheel. Finally, the fog was starting to lift. This was the family she'd built with Ron, and the town they'd served together to raise that family in. She loved them both and was not about to let a dead man's threat or the very real threat of a drug ring harm either one.

She smiled for the first time all day.

Chapter 15
by Carmen Will

Glory awoke in complete darkness, her heart pounding and her nightgown soaked with sweat. The clock on her nightstand said 2:00 a.m., and she'd just had the worst nightmare of her life, which was saying a lot because she'd had more nightmares than she could count in the few days since Tom Rankin's death. The timing of the dream was surprising, though, because when she'd gone to bed last night, she'd felt secure and at peace. Her boys had all vowed to do what they could to help her get to the bottom of the mystery surrounding Tom's murder, and she knew that they'd come through for her. They always did.

After slipping into her robe and slippers, she went downstairs to the kitchen, put a pan of milk on the stove to warm, and lifted a Wedgwood cocoa pot from its shelf. She'd found the white fluted ironstone pot and six matching cups a month ago and hadn't had the heart to put them up for sale at Glory Days. Ever since she'd been a little girl, a steaming cup of hot chocolate in the middle of the night had been able to quell the stubborn vestiges of any bad dream. She arranged the pot, cup, and a few shortbread cookies on a tray and headed back up to her bedroom.

When she noticed light filtering into the hallway from the gap under Chance's door, she set the tray on the hallway table and knocked softly. "Sweetheart, are you awake?"

"I'm awake, Mom. Come in."

She nudged open the door. "What are you still doing up at this hour?"

Chance was sitting at his desk, both hands on his computer keyboard. "I tried to sleep but couldn't, so I gave up and decided to do some research. What about you?"

"Another nightmare." She retrieved the tray and set it on the desk next to her son's computer. "So I made you some cocoa."

He laughed. "Don't fib, Mom. Only you would have a craving for hot chocolate in the middle of a July heat wave. But if you insist—" He poured some cocoa into the cup and took a sip. "Want to tell me about your nightmare?"

Glory sat on the edge of his bed. "You know as well as I do that no one ever wants to hear about someone else's dreams. It's worse than being forced to look at their vacation photos."

Chance shrugged. "I actually like hearing about people's dreams—especially the scary ones."

Glory took a cookie from the tray and narrowed her eyes at him. "You really want to hear about it?"

"Yeah, I do. Maybe just the short version, though."

Glory took a bite of the cookie and chewed thoughtfully. "Your dad and I were on a Ferris wheel...like the one at the carnival. He was wearing a red wig and a clown suit."

"Dad in a clown suit? No way."

"Hey, you asked for this—let me finish. He said, 'Glory, you have to go back to the beginning.' Slade Rankin told me pretty much the same thing when I was at his restaurant with Connie the other day."

"And...?"

"And then I heard a shot—and your father died right there on the Ferris wheel, just like Tom Rankin did."

"And then...?" Chance repeated, his voice tinged with impatience.

"Lilly was on the ground holding her cell phone up toward me. 'You have to take this call,' she said. 'It's a matter of life and death!' And then I woke up."

"Uh, I hate to tell you, Mom, but that nightmare isn't all that scary. It's actually kind of funny—except for the Dad getting shot part."

Glory smiled weakly. "I guess you had to be there."

"So what do you think it means? They say that dreams are a form of self-communication. So what are you trying to tell yourself?"

She shrugged. "I wish I knew. I don't understand this thing about going back to the beginning. The carnival has already moved on from Rainbow's End to some other town, so there's nothing left to go back to but an empty lot. Next week, the Ladies' Guild will be holding its Farmers' Market there to raise money for local charities. And what on earth was Lilly doing in my dream? What was the important phone call she wanted me to take? I have no idea." Her gaze rested on Chance's computer monitor. "What about your research? Did you find anything?"

He tilted the screen toward her. "Come take a look."

Glory walked over to him and peered over his shoulder. "A website for Nutmeg, LLC? The agency that handled staffing for the carnival at the county fair?"

Chance leaned back in his chair to give his mother a better view. "Yup. I've been doing a little digging into it. It's a fake company, Mom. They have a bunch of social media links—you know, Facebook, Twitter, Instagram—but all the links are dead. Nutmeg lists a BBB Accreditation on their website, but that's fake, too. I entered the company's address on Google Earth, and this is what I came up with." He pulled up a grid map that filled the screen.

Glory squinted at the network of lines and points, which appeared surprisingly complex for a neighborhood in Rainbow's End. "There's the address, but I can't see the building."

"Right. That's because there *is* no building. The last business assigned to that address was a hardware store that burned to the ground five years ago. Nutmeg, LLC's address is a vacant lot."

Glory shook her head slowly. "What does it mean?"

"It means that whoever staffed the carnival went to a lot of trouble to hide their true identity. My friend Clara—the one I told you about who works for Parks and Rec—told me that someone from Nutmeg, LLC contacted them about staffing the carnival a month before it was scheduled to open and was told to go ahead. Unfortunately, no one from Parks and Rec checked into the company's background."

"So who's behind Nutmeg, LLC?"

Chance shook his head. "I don't know, Mom." He switched off his computer, got up from his chair, and put an arm around Glory's shoulder. "I think we both need to get some sleep. Maybe things will make more sense in the morning." He handed the cocoa tray, complete with used cup, back to his mother. "I think you need this more than I do."

Glory managed a tired smile. "Thanks for your help, sweetheart. I don't know what I'd do without you…or your brothers. I'm sure we'll have some answers soon."

But the morning brought only more questions. Tyler showed up at the house early, and his face was grim. He poured himself a cup of coffee and sat down at the table with Glory. "Remember how Joey thought the stuffed bear from the carnival was filled with drugs?"

Glory nodded.

"Well, he was wrong. It wasn't filled with drugs. It was stuffed with cash—two-hundred and fifty thousand dollars, mostly fifty- and hundred-dollar bills. Tom Rankin must have done something pretty spectacular to earn that much money."

"But I'm the one who ended up with it. Tom gave me that bear. It doesn't make sense that he'd do that if he knew it was stuffed with cash."

Tyler sighed. "Mom, I don't think Tom ever intended for you to go home with the bear. You were his cover. You know…for show."

Glory frowned. "You think Tom was planning to walk me to my car, and instead of kissing me goodnight, he was going to grab the bear and take off with it?"

"Maybe. Or maybe he was planning to take you into his confidence—tell you about the cash and where it came from."

Glory shook her head. "I think you're wrong about that. I also think Tom took a liking to me right away. He wouldn't have used me as some sort of shill. How does Ned think the money fits into all this?"

"He believes that it's drug money, but we still don't know where it came from, or who that shooting gallery attendant was and why he gave the bear to Rankin." He paused to take a long sip of coffee, and when he continued, his eyes carefully avoided Glory's. "There's something else. The chief and I reviewed the security footage of the shop's front entrance from the day you received the cashier's check and the deed to Scott Ashford's property. No one touched the mailbox that day except for the mail carrier and Lilly."

"Are you sure?"

"Positive. We even reviewed footage from the camera mounted outside the toy store next to your shop. Your mailbox is clearly visible from the store's camera, and the footage is consistent with what we saw on the antique shop's security feed."

"I don't get it," said Glory. "There was no postmark on the envelope, so *someone* had to have put it in my mailbox. It didn't just magically appear there."

Tyler cleared his throat. The envelope that Lilly gave you, Mom…it was clear from the security DVDs—both yours and the toy store's—that it was in her hand before she reached the mailbox. She slipped that envelope into the stack of mail before she gave it to you."

"But why would Lilly lie and tell me she'd found it with the rest of the mail?"

"I have no idea, but I think I should go into the shop with you today so we can ask her about it."

Just as Glory was about to respond, the doorbell rang, and she made a move to answer it.

Tyler extended both arms to signal her to sit back down. "Stay right there, Mom. I'll get it."

Glory heard some hushed conversation in the living room, and a minute later Tyler returned to the kitchen with Chief Walker right behind him. The chief removed his hat and greeted Glory with a nod. "How are you holding up?" He pointed a finger at Tyler. "I hope this one's been taking good care of you."

"All four of my boys are taking good care of me, Ned."

"Well," the chief responded, "you raised them right. That's for sure."

Glory laughed. "Ron may have had a little something to do with that."

When she noticed the chief and Tyler exchange an uncomfortable glance, she said, "Ned, I'm sure that you didn't just stop in to say good morning. Is there something you came here to tell me?"

"As a matter of fact, there is. Glory, Slade Rankin's dead. His sister left him alone at Nutmeg's for a few hours to run some errands, and when she got back, she found him at the bottom of the stairs. His neck had been broken."

The grim announcement flooded Glory's mind with a montage of happy memories...memories of a brief but fun-filled time spent with Slade, when they'd both been young and in love, when he'd been handsome, smart, and fun-loving, before drugs had turned his brain to mush and his body to that of an old man.

"Was it an accident?" asked Glory, her voice shaking.

"We don't know yet," said Ned. "I've got my forensic guy at the scene right now. We'll have to send anything he finds to the crime lab in Montpelier. And we won't know the results for at least a few weeks."

Glory buried her face in her hands. "First Tom, then Elise Ashford, and now Slade." She looked up, her gaze darting from Ned, to Tyler, and back to Ned again. "Three people dead—four, if we count Ron. Why? And who's going to be next?"

Chance, who'd been listening from the dining room hallway, entered the kitchen and knelt on the floor next to Glory. He took her hand into his. "Mom, you should close the shop for a few days. I heard what Tyler said. You need to take some time off, and Lilly can't be trusted."

Glory shook her head. Tears were flooding her eyes when she said, "I can't—I can't afford to close the shop."

"Then I'll run it for you," said Chance, "just for a few days—until we have some answers. I can do it, Mom...and Joey can help out, too. We've worked in the shop practically since we were able to walk."

She shook her head. "No." She stood and reached out to give Chance a hug. "I appreciate your offer, but I'm not going to let anyone keep me from doing the things I love to do. I'm not going to let anyone stop me from living." She directed her gaze to Tyler. "Can we leave now? Lilly's opening the shop this morning, and I want to talk to her before the first customer shows up. I have to give her a chance to explain herself."

A few minutes later, Tyler and Glory pulled into the small parking lot behind the shop fifteen minutes ahead of opening time. They found Lilly in the stockroom, looking for items to replace those that had been sold during the fire sale.

She greeted them with a bright smile. "Morning, guys!" Then she noted the looks on their faces. "What's the matter? What happened?"

"Slade Rankin's dead," said Tyler, "and we have a few questions to ask you."

Lilly's eyes grew wide. "That's awful, and I'm sorry, but what could I possibly know about it? You don't think I had anything to do with it, do you?!"

"Of course not," said Glory. "What we have to talk to you about has nothing to do with Slade Rankin. Chief Walker and Tyler reviewed security footage of the front of the shop, and they saw something on it that needs an explanation."

"From you," added Tyler.

"What do you want me to explain?" asked Lilly, her voice cracking.

"Why you lied to me about that envelope for Scott Ashford," said Glory. "You said you'd found it with the rest of the mail that morning. But you're the one who placed that envelope in the mailbox. What do you have to do with all this, Lilly? Where did you get that envelope? Who gave it to you?" With an angry swipe of her hand, Glory brushed a tear from her face. "I thought I could trust you."

"But you can!" said Lilly. "You *can* trust me! I—I found the envelope on the counter next to the cash register when I came into the shop that morning. I knew it hadn't been there when I left the day before, because I would have seen it when I was counting out the drawer. I—must have forgotten to lock up when I left— the door was unlocked when I arrived the next morning—and someone must have come into the shop during the night and left the envelope on the counter." Tears rolled down her cheeks. "I was afraid to tell you, so I pretended that the envelope came with the rest of the mail."

Tyler's eyes reflected his skepticism as he studied Lilly's face. "The security footage didn't show anyone entering the shop that night after closing. So how do you explain the envelope ending up on the counter? The Invisible Man? A ghost?"

She shook her head. "I can't explain it." Her cell phone rang, and she glanced at it while wiping tears from her eyes. "I've been waiting for this call. It's from my cousin Sharon. I asked her to do some digging into the Ashfords. She might have learned something important."

Tyler nodded. "Go ahead and take the call. But our conversation isn't over yet. I have a few more questions."

Tyler and Glory went out to the front of the shop, and Glory unlocked the door to welcome a few customers who'd been waiting outside. As she set about straightening the shelves, she abruptly turned to Tyler, who was standing near the door to the stockroom. "Oh my gosh." Her face had gone white.

"What's wrong, Mom? Are you all right?"

Without a word, Glory joined him at the door and stared at Lilly, who had been pacing back and forth past the door of the stockroom, pausing now and again in the opening, still engrossed in her discussion with Sharon. "Oh my gosh," she repeated.

Tyler swiveled to follow his mother's gaze. "What? What is it, Mom?"

"That night at the carnival—there was a young woman on her cell phone. She was standing near the base of the Ferris wheel. I remember her because she seemed so angry. She was screaming at someone on her phone, so loudly that I could hear her from the top of the ride." She turned back to Tyler and said, "And right after Tom was murdered, I saw her take off and lose herself in the crowd. I only had a side view of her, but seeing Lilly on her phone just now—Tyler, I'm ninety-nine percent sure that the woman on the phone that night was Lilly."

Chapter 16
by Leslie Stansfield

The bell on the door jangled again. Glory turned and saw Tyler's partner Alice walk in. Glory and Tyler exchanged glances that indicated they would continue their discussion later. Glory wasn't going to start blurting things out in Alice's presence.

"Hey, I thought I saw the two of you in here," Alice said. "Tyler, I've been looking for you. The chief wants to have us sit in on a briefing with the FBI. I was going to radio you when I saw you here. The scuttlebutt is that the FBI did tests to try and calculate the trajectory of the bullet that killed Tom Rankin."

Lilly peeked her head around the corner of the storeroom door, still on the phone. "Sorry, family nonsense. I'll be off shortly." Seeing Alice, she waved and said, "Hey, Alice. You might as well know Glory and Tyler now think I had something to do with that mysterious letter getting in here. More to come." She waved again and ducked back into the small room.

Alice's eyebrows went up and then came down in a frown. Cocking her head at her partner, she asked, "Wanna share?"

Tyler filled her in on the fact that while they'd seen no one on the security footage of the front door the night of the shooting, someone had left that threatening letter at Glory Days—and that Lilly claimed she'd found the letter on the counter upon her arrive the next morning. She'd just too afraid to admit it because she'd assumed she'd carelessly left the shop unlocked overnight and didn't want to tell Glory. So instead, she'd bent the truth, saying the letter had been in the mailbox outside, mixed in with the other letters. But if that was true, who could've left the letter on the counter? It didn't fit. An invisible person didn't put it there.

"You've got a point . . ." Alice hesitated a bit "Still, I can't see Lilly doing that. It doesn't seem to fit what we know about her."

"Well, there's more," Glory added, feeling a little bit defensive. She filled Alice in about seeing Lilly by the Ferris wheel just before Tom had been shot. She'd just finished explaining when Lilly came out of the stockroom.

"How are you, Alice? I hope you're—" Lilly stopped mid-sentence. "What now?" she asked, an edge of annoyance in her voice. "You're all looking at me like I shot the man!"

"I saw you," Glory said quietly. She found herself glancing around the room, unable to bring herself to look at Lilly.

"Saw me shoot him?" Lilly scoffed. "There's no possible way that could be true." Her voice was starting to get a little shrill. "I cannot even count the number of people at the carnival who saw me there with my kids that night. What's more, I'm sure plenty of people heard me screaming on the phone when my kids didn't meet me at the bench near the Ferris wheel at the time we'd agreed on. Those two are grounded not only until the cows come home, but until the cows brush their teeth and are in bed for the night!"

Glory looked up and realized that Tyler and Alice were smiling now, but Lilly didn't seem to notice.

"And by the way, I don't even *own* a gun. And you know me, Glory. I would never—"

"Hold up there, Lilly," Tyler said, raising his hands. "Mom only meant she saw you *at the carnival*. Not that you killed anyone. Just simmer down. This case has got everyone on edge. We're not accustomed to murder in Rainbow's End."

The door bells jangled again and Cameron came into the shop. "Hey, all. Town meeting?" He looked at Lilly, who was still frowning and red in the face. "Well, it looks like I walked in at a bad time. What gives?"

"Oh nothing much," said Lilly, crossing her arms. "Your mother and brother here just think I planted the letter and shot Tom Rankin."

Glory could hear the hurt in Lilly's voice and felt a little ashamed. How could she have thought, even for a moment, that Lilly had played any part in this madness? Tyler interrupted her thoughts.

"I was just saying that so many people have died recently in this small town that it has everyone on edge."

"Yeah," Cameron agreed. "Mom goes out on one little date, and half the town ends up dead."

Glory cut her eyes to her son and saw him grinning at his brother who burst out laughing.

"Good point, Cam. Mom, we need to take you off the dating circuit. Too risky."

Everyone laughed, except Glory, who put her hands on her hips. "Yuck it up, everyone. You weren't the one sitting next to a dead man."

"As I was saying before, I can't explain how that letter got on the counter," Lilly said, much calmer now. "I wish I could. I don't blame you for wondering if I put it there. I'd think that too. However, we do have a back door, remember. Plenty of people can pick a lock."

Tyler nodded. "Good point."

"Wait just one moment," Lilly said, darting in the back. There was a whizzing noise and then a ripping sound. With a long piece of wrapping paper trailing behind her, Lilly scurried back into the main room. She quickly removed a lace tablecloth from a long oval table and put the wrapping paper, design side down, on top.

"Everyone take a seat," she demanded. "In all the mystery books I've read, the cops write down notes on a white board. We don't have one of those, so this will have to do!" She turned and yanked the pens out of the cup by the cash register and tossed them on the table. "Let's have at this. We need to see what we've got."

"Whoa," Tyler said, alarm in his voice. "Let's not get carried away. Chief Walker will blow a gasket if he finds out about this. Bad idea. *Very* bad idea."

"Can't you humor us for an hour?" Cameron asked. "The woman has a point. Is there any harm in just seeing what we all come up with together?"

Glory saw Tyler look down. She knew he was embarrassed. This was no laughing matter to him, and he was a police officer—and Chief Walker was his boss.

"Look, a few minutes ago you were actually all suspicious of me," said Lilly. "Now, I didn't kill anyone—and I want to be part of the solution. It can't hurt to try putting our heads together."

"Okay, point taken," Alice said. "But you all have to understand that there will be certain things that Tyler and I can't share. In two hours, there's an FBI briefing."

The little door bells jingle-jangled again, and in came Chief Walker.

For the love of Pete! Glory thought. *Does anyone come into this store to actually shop?*

"I was just passing by on my way for coffee, and I looked in and spotted all of you. Something tells me this is no coincidence. Something's up and I know it, so you might as well spill whatever it is."

Everyone started talking at once. Glory was trying to say that it was only a coincidence that they were all in her shop, Lilly was squawking about the letter, Tyler and Alice were trying to calm everyone down, and Cameron was explaining that Glory was no longer allowed to date.

"Whoa!" shouted the chief. "Slow it all down. I get that Lilly is being accused of the letter business. I think I heard something about this little meeting here being unplanned, and," he said with a big grin, "Glory is off the dating circuit. Did I miss anything?"

"Just that I see no harm in everyone sitting at the table and us writing down our ideas," Lilly said. "I know we aren't detectives, but it doesn't hurt to review the facts anyway."

Chief Walker's eyebrows shot up, almost meeting his receding hairline. He paused, scanning the group and stopping on Alice and Tyler. The room was so quiet that Glory wondered if the others could hear her heart pounding.

"And you two thought…" He looked at his officers.

"They told us not to get involved with the investigation," Glory quickly said.

Lilly cleared her throat. "I just thought that since we're all here talking about the situation anyway, we might as well compare thoughts."

Another pregnant pause. Glory could feel the tension in the room as they all looked at the chief, waiting for his response.

Finally, he blew out a deep breath and extended an arm to the table. "You all might as well sit and have at it, then. Better in front of my face than behind by back.

But understand, we aren't giving any classified information away. We can't share what we can't share. Got it?"

There was a collective whoosh of air. Glory realized they'd all been holding their breath until that moment. They took seats around the table, and Lilly handed Chief Walker a black marker.

"Okay, let's start back at the beginning, with you, Glory. You met Tom at the Ferris wheel—" he began.

"Sort of," said Glory. "He was leaning on the fence by the ride. I just knew it was him. Not sure how I did, but I did." Glory could see Tom so clearly in her mind.

"Okay. Next was the shooting gallery. He won that and took the bear as his prize. Did he pick it out? Did the man hand it to him?"

"Well, it wasn't one of the prizes hanging up. The man reached for something high and Tom pointed to the bear in the corner and said he wanted that one. The man said that was just for show, but Tom insisted. The man seemed a little flustered, but I thought it was because he didn't think Tom would win. That was clear from the beginning. It didn't seem strange to me because I just assumed few people ever win those things."

"What do you mean, it was clear from the beginning? What makes you say that?" Ned asked.

"The operator said that no one hits four or more. When Tom did, he looked shocked."

As the chief started writing, Cameron said, "Maybe Tom wasn't the one who was supposed to get the bear. Maybe that bear was meant for someone else."

"It's possible," said Alice. "Maybe Tom had actually been watching the shooting gallery for a while. Maybe even over a few nights. We have no idea what he did or where he was before he met Glory."

"Well," Glory said, thinking back, "he did say he didn't realize what he'd gotten himself into. Maybe he really wasn't the one the bear was meant for. Maybe he intercepted it."

The chief wrote down "Bear intercepted?" on the sheet of wrapping paper.

"Who suggested the ride—you or him?" Tyler asked.

"I did. I love the Ferris wheel."

"Okay, so that means that the timing of the killing wasn't premeditated, right?" said Lilly. "Whoever did it had to be watching and waiting for the right time."

"The FBI is going to tell us about their findings this afternoon," Chief Walker said as he wrote. "I won't know for sure until then, but my money's on that bullet making a downward trajectory. I don't believe it came from the ground."

"Oh, that reminds me. I think I stepped on a rifle scope," Glory added. I thought it was a kaleidoscope at the time, but I think it was actually a rifle scope."

"Ah, yes," the chief added, writing. He looked around the table. "Lilly, we're going to need more pens."

"Got it," Lilly said. "Oh—let's not forget the black widow spider drawing."

"Got it," Alice said, uncapping her pen. "Do we have any ideas what that meant?"

"I thought it referred to the fact that Ron was dead and now Tom Rankin. I thought it was a nasty shot at me," said Glory.

"Well it's also a ride at the carnival," said Lilly. "It's the reason my kids were late meeting me. They didn't want to get off the thing."

"Excellent point," Chief Walker said, nodding at Lilly. "That one got right by us."

"And then there's the blasted letter," Lilly added. "I don't know how it got here. I swear I don't, but it was on the counter."

"Well," Cameron said, standing up and stretching. "There's the back door, like you said earlier. And of course, three buildings in a row here share the same basement."

Glory felt a jolt. The basement! She shared the basement with the buildings on either side of Glory Days. Why hadn't she thought of that sooner? "I completely forgot that. Cameron, you're a genius. It's a whole new possibility. And yes, someone could have picked the back lock as well. Lilly, I'm sorry I doubted you even for a moment. I'm just a mess."

Lilly nodded, and Glory knew she wasn't quite forgiven, but it was a start. She would work more on that later.

"Then we have the murder of Elise Ashford and the question of the deed. That has to play into this somehow. It can't be coincidence that Tom dies, I get a letter—possibly from him—with the deed and the check, and then she turns up dead too."

"Yup, hold on," Tyler said, writing furiously. "Dang it, this pen is running out of ink." Alice threw him hers and Lilly quickly gave her another one.

"Tyler," Cameron said, "leave plenty of blank space around that part. We need to come back to it. It's a whole mess on its own."

Glory sighed. "And then there's Slade." She felt a pang of sadness. "Slade is now dead, and he has something to do with this."

Alice jumped up and moved to another space on the wrapping paper. She wrote "SLADE!" and boxed it in.

Ned Walker stood up and walked around the table, nodding. "Good, good. This is helpful," he mumbled. "Lots to fill in, but this is good." He stopped and looked at Glory. "Let's focus on the Elise Ashford murder for a minute. What do we have?"

"There was the envelope left on the counter. In the envelope was a ten-thousand-dollar check made out to Mr. Ashford, the deed to the property, and a note telling me to deliver them to him because the life of someone close to me was at stake," said Glory.

"Not necessarily a member of our family," Cameron added. "I just realized that. Someone you are close to. That opens things up a bit."

Glory felt a small wave of relief. Perhaps the note hadn't even been referring to her family. It could be a friend. Her stomach turned. It could be Lilly. Lilly had lots of historic connections in town.

"Could it be Lilly?" she blurted. "Maybe that's why it was left here at the shop. Lilly's family has been here in town forever!"

Lilly swallowed. "I'll ask my family if there's any connection between us and that property."

The chief looked at his watch. "We need to wrap this up. Let's get down what we have on Slade and call it a day for now."

Everyone turned to Glory. She closed her eyes and blew out a long, slow breath. She needed to think back. "Connie and I went together to the Nutmeg. It was closed. Slade was there, and he was very cryptic. He told me I had to give *it* to them or I would suffer. I have no idea what the *it* is. He told me I had to lie down where all the ladders start. I think he said something about it being in the rag and bone shop of the heart. Yes, I think that's what he said. He said I didn't want to be a black widow."

"Okay," said Alice. "Maybe it's not the ride. Maybe there is a connection between Chief Lockhart's death and this."

Glory nodded, feeling sicker. "Slade knew all about the deed and the money. He knew, of course, about Tom's death."

Tyler's, Alice's, and the chief's radios squawked at once. The chief yanked his from his belt and pushed the button. "Go ahead," he said.

"There's a report of shots fired at the Robertson home. Neighbors called in an active shooter. Shots went through the Robertson's big front window and the Robertsons seem to be shooting back. Cars on their way there now, Chief."

"Block off the road. On our way," Chief Walker barked. "Let's move," he said to Tyler and Alice.

The door shut behind them, and Cameron, Glory, and Lilly were left to stare at each other. Glory remembered her last conversation with Connie. Were she and Max really helping Tom with an undercover FBI case? She wasn't going to bring that up now, but she'd talk to Ned about it later.

"Mom," Cameron said gently, "your hands are shaking. Are you okay? I know Connie is one of your closest friends, and Connie and Max set up the date between you and Tom."

Glory looked down. Her hands were indeed shaking.

"I think it's time for coffee," Lilly said as a few customers walked into the store.

Cameron folded over the sheet of paper, hiding their notes, and put the cup of pens on top of it. He smiled at his mother and patted her hand. "I'll take this with me when I go," he said, nodding at the folded paper. "It's safer at my house than here. Next time I see Tyler, I'll give it to him."

Glory nodded. She as ready to get up and help her customers—glad there was someone here shopping. Maybe she would work on the display out front as well.

She needed to keep busy. Sitting and stewing was useless. Lilly put a cup of hot coffee in her hand and Glory smiled at her. Lilly winked, making Glory's heart feel a little lighter.

"Come out front and look at the display with me," she said to Cameron. "Maybe an extra set of eyes will help. The judging is tomorrow."

They wandered out the front door. Glory took a moment to look at the other shops. Everyone had done an amazing job this year. There was certainly lots of competition. Cynthia's toy shop looked adorable with wagons set up like a July 4th parade—the dolls and stuffed animals waving flags.

"Competition is tough this year," Cameron said, echoing his mother's thoughts. "Although, I think the vintage feel gives you an advantage. It's homey."

Glory nodded. She wanted to do something fun with the display. What could she do that would say summer fun in a patriotic, lighthearted way? She thought about what she had in the store. "I've got it. Come with me!"

With Cameron at her heels, she waved to Lilly on her way through the shop, then threw open the door to the stockroom closet. It was a very deep closet, lined with shelves containing things to help with their displays. She tugged out the female mannequin and handed it to Cameron.

"Mom, she's naked!" he wailed, laughing.

"Well, just shut your eyes then!" She opened a dresser drawer filled with old clothes and began tossing things out. "Put this on her!" She jogged to the back of the store.

Lilly was holding the door open for the customers just leaving the shop, and Glory was glad to see they were laden down with packages. Lilly shut the door and spotted Glory. "Do you need help?"

"Yes, please. Grab me that pram over there and follow me out front."

A half-hour later, the three of them stood in front of the store to admire their handiwork. Slumped in an exhausted position on a chair, dressed in a vintage red, white, and blue dress, was the female mannequin with one hand on the pram. Blocks, dolls, and stuffed animals were strewn near the wheels as if they'd just been flung out. In the mannequin's other hand was a small flag. She truly looked like a bushed mother at a parade who could barely manage one last *whoopee*. Her white, wide-brimmed hat was cockeyed and one of her red shoes sat askew on her foot.

Lilly laughed. "That's exactly how I felt after that carnival. I went there two nights with my kids. They loved it. For me, the first night was fun, but the second was awful. They met their friends there and wanted to ride some of the rides by themselves. I thought it would be fun to have a few minutes to myself. And it was—until they were ten minutes late and I had to start calling their cell phones, which they didn't pick up on the first try. I panicked. I was almost in tears. On the second try they acted like I was interrupting their fun. The other kids' parents were just as mad. By the time I got home, I felt like *that!*" She pointed at the mannequin. "Bravo to you, Glory. I love it."

"Mom, it's the perfect touch. I think that's the part that will put you over the top this year. I agree with Lilly. Kudos to you." Cameron looked down at his phone and frowned. "We better go inside and turn on your television. I just got a news alert." He waved his phone. "Two other towns have sent in police. The FBI is at the scene. I'm guessing it's the Robertson house. They're saying there might be a hostage situation."

Chapter 17
by Julie Seedorf

"It was a false alarm, folks!" Kaitlyn Nash, the reporter from WRKB news in Rainbow's End was just announcing as the television blared to life in the antique shop.

"False alarm?" Glory asked. "How can that be? We heard Ned get the call."

Cameron hushed his mother. "Shh! She's explaining."

"Yes, you heard me right, a false alarm. What was thought to be shots fired through the front picture window of a home in Rainbow's End actually turned out to be an explosive going off *inside* the house, blowing out the window and causing a store of ammunition inside to explode, which led the police to conclude they were being fired at. This is according to a statement made by FBI agent, Joe Sherman. Local chief of police, Ned Walker, who just arrived at the scene corroborated that statement. WRKB has also confirmed there were no hostages involved. A neighbor mistakenly thought he heard a call for help coming from inside the home before the explosion detonated. At this time, all we know is that the homeowners, Connie and Max Robertson of Rainbow's End, were not home at the time of the explosion and no one was hurt. Tune in to the evening news for more developments in the case."

Glory switched the television off. "I need to go over to the Robertsons' house and be there for them when they come home. This will be a huge shock. I know I've had my suspicions that things with them are not as they are supposed to be, but they've been my friends for years and they helped me so much when Ron died."

"Are you sure, Glory?" asked Lilly. "It's awfully strange for their house to explode out of the blue. And why did they have so much ammunition stockpiled in there?"

"I don't think Tyler and Chief Walker will be happy if you run over there and interfere in the investigation," Cameron added.

Glory opened the door and stepped outside before answering. "They're my friends until proven otherwise and I'm going to treat them as such. Please close the shop for me, would you?"

"Of course. You go ahead." Lilly shooed her out the door. "You go too, Cam. I have things taken care of here."

"Mom, what are you doing here?" Tyler met Glory just as she was about to duck under the crime scene tape.

"I wanted to be here when Connie and Max get back. They're going to be devastated to find their home in shambles." Glory's gaze moved to the house that the Robertson's had loved and taken care of for so many years. It was still sizzling in places.

"Maybe not as devastated as you think."

"What do you mean by that?"

"Mom, has Connie said anything to you about where they might have been going? Maybe on a trip out of town?"

"No, not a thing. Why?"

"Maybe you should sit down for this." Ned Walker had come up from behind, and after hearing their conversation, took Glory by the arm and led her back to her car. He opened the passenger door and indicated she should get in and sit down.

"Ned, you're scaring me." Glory took a seat, leaving her legs dangling outside the car. She sought Tyler's reassurance, but he was staring at the ground.

"There's no easy way to tell you this, but after we got inside the house we found some things that tell us that Connie and Max are not who we thought they were."

Glory sighed. "I know that, but I've been hoping it wasn't true. Connie said Tom Rankin was FBI and had asked for their help in getting in touch with me. She said he wanted to grill me on what I knew about Ron's cases. I wondered if it was true at the time and did a little investigating on my own. So you're confirming this now?"

Tyler lifted his head and looked at Ned.

Seeing the look, Glory asked, "What? What is it?"

Tyler took Glory's hand in his. "By the evidence we found in a concealed room in their basement, it's clear they weren't *helping* Tom in any way—or the FBI, for that matter. They were undercover members of the drug ring. Of course, they'd set themselves up as outstanding members of the community so we wouldn't suspect. We had no reason to look at them as being part of the problem."

The expression on Ned's face was grave. "Glory, Connie killed Ron. And it looks like they also were responsible for Slade's death."

Glory gasped, her hand flying to her mouth. She hesitated before speaking, feeling suddenly breathless. "Connie! Connie killed Ron? How can that be? She and Max were our friends. Connie was my rock when Ron was killed. Are you sure?"

"We are. They left a journal with dates and times that chronicled their business and what they had to do. I don't think they ever thought they would get caught," Ned answered. "And clearly they thought all the evidence would have been destroyed in this explosion." He looked back at the remains of the house. "But the Rainbow's End Fire Department was too efficient for that."

"Slade was deep undercover, unbeknownst to Tom," said Tyler. "Apparently, neither brother knew what the other was up to. Dad was on his way to see Slade when he was killed. I know that because we found hidden documentation in a safe in the Robertsons' basement too. That probably also explains why Slade was killed. We don't know why Dad was on his way to see him. It could've been just to check on his wellbeing since he had problems with drugs. Or maybe Dad knew it was all a cover and Slade wasn't really strung out at all— maybe it was all an act and they were working together. We don't know. But according to what we found in the secret room, Connie was the person Dad stopped on the road that night. She was waiting for him and then she shot him."

Glory felt the world slipping out from under her. She burst into tears.

The men let her cry for a few minutes and then Tyler said, "Why don't you let me drive you home. Then I'll come back and help finish up here at the scene. One of the other patrolmen can pick me up at your house."

Glory removed his hand from her arm, "No, I'll be fine. So Connie and Max killed Slade and Tom too?"

"By the looks of it, they killed Slade. After he talked to you in Connie's presence, they suspected he was not the druggie he seemed to be and they felt that put them in danger. They had a strange quirk of writing out the details of the murders in their records." Ned shook his head. "It's almost as if they relished what they did and wanted to keep the gritty details for posterity."

"I can't believe it," said Glory, wiping tears from her cheeks.

"I know," said Ned. "I'm a trained lawman, and I would have never guessed this of Max and Connie."

Glory sniffed. "Did they kill Tom Rankin, too?"

"We don't think so," said Tyler. "There appear to be more people involved. It seems someone called Flopsy had the job of doing away with Tom. We think that's a pet name and Flopsy may very well be someone we know."

"I still don't understand. I've been to their house thousands of times. Connie was my best friend. I never saw anything—any hint that this was going on," said Glory.

"Mom, you were married to Dad. You understand secrecy in investigations." Tyler put a hand on her shoulder. "And you also understand it's vital that we keep this under wraps. You can't tell anyone if we share this with you, not even the family, do you understand?"

"Glory, we're willing to let you in on what we know," said Ned, lowering his voice. "Even against our better judgment. But please don't let those FBI men know we breathed a word of this to you or they won't let us continue to consult on the case." He paused. "The thing is, I feel your life could be in danger, too." He glanced over to where Agent Steele was standing.

"Get in the car," Tyler said. "I'll take you to the shop and explain the rest on the way. Chief, would you send Alice over in a squad car to pick me up later?"

Ned patted the car and said in a loud voice so the FBI agents would hear, "I'm sure the Robertsons are fine. We'll let you know, Glory, when they come home."

Tyler inched the car away from the curb. "We think someone set the explosion and purposely put the ammunition close enough so that it too would go off. The arson investigators are here now." He nodded toward the vehicles that were just pulling up at the house.

"I can't believe this. I still just can't believe this." Glory pounded her hand down on the dash. "Why would Max kill his own friend? Why did Connie tell me this convoluted story about helping Tom? What did she have to gain?"

"She may have thought you knew something. Connie and Max may be tied to that deed and the letter that was left at your shop for Winifred Scott Ashford in ways we don't yet understand. Whoever left it possibly didn't have time to take it all the way out to his place. We just aren't sure yet. And then, remember, you and Connie visited the Nutmeg and Slade. Whose idea was it to go there?"

"It's my fault Slade is dead," Glory muttered.

"How did you come up with that one, Mom?"

"I took Connie to the Nutmeg. Maybe Slade didn't know about Connie being part of the drug ring. Otherwise, why would he give me the clue?"

"Are you sure he gave you what he intended? Maybe he recognized Connie and told you what he did to throw her off. Or, he might have sensed he was in danger and in spite of Connie being there took the chance of giving you the clue. I guess we may never know."

Tyler turned into the antique store's parking lot.

"There's Lilly! What do I tell her? Is there still a chance she's part of all this—since she found the letter, I mean?"

"Just tell her that Max and Connie's house is in shambles. It will come out in the papers that it was a gas leak for those in the community who're looking for information. One more thing, we found a cache of drugs in the hidden room in the basement along with an extensive underground tunnel that leads under the police department and elsewhere. That's the way they must have been funneling their merchandise. The only reason I'm telling you this is because you need to watch your back. What Slade told you could or could not be the truth, but if it is, whoever's still out there might figure you're a threat to them and your life could be in danger. And remember Connie and Max are still out there somewhere too."

The passenger door of the car was wrenched open.

"Glory, are you okay? Why is Tyler bringing you back here? Were Connie and Max hurt? They were in the house after all, weren't they? I can see you've been crying." Lilly hugged Glory.

"Look what I found!" Tyler, who'd hopped out of the driver's seat and walked around the side of the car had stopped and bent to pull something out of the back seat. Now he was carrying a black and white cat whose hair appeared to be singed in places. The cat snuggled down deeper in Tyler's arms. "We had a stowaway! He looks like he's been in an explosion."

Chapter 18
by Lorrie Holmgren

They hurried into the shop and Glory reached out to touch the cat's fur. "Oh no! Poor Mr. Whiskers. He's Connie's cat." The Persian's formerly long and luxurious fur was now short, singed, and reeking of smoke. His signature whiskers were gone and his gray paws pink. The cat looked at her with reproachful green eyes as if blaming her for the whole deplorable situation.

"What should I do with him, Mom?" Tyler asked. "I'd hate to take him to the animal shelter after what he's been through."

"No, don't do that. I'll keep him here in the shop for now." *Probably forever*, Glory thought. She tried to take Mr. Whiskers but he wiggled out of Tyler's arms, jumped to the floor and hid under a Queen Anne armchair.

"I have to get back to the crime scene," Tyler said. "Where's Cam?"

Lilly gave a little wave. "He went back to your house, Glory. He said he wanted to start supper for you."

"Are you okay to get home?" asked Ty. "The squad car's here for me."

"Of course. I'm fine." Glory clasped her trembling hands behind her back. It had been a terrible shock to hear about the explosion and Connie and Max's guilt, but life had made Glory a strong woman and she knew she'd be fine. "I have some bills and other paperwork to catch up on here at the shop. You go on back to work."

Tyler hugged her and jogged out to the patrol car. Glory knew she was lucky to have such devoted, decent sons.

She went into the restroom and poured water into a small porcelain bowl decorated in an antique rose pattern and placed it in front of the chair where Mr. Whiskers was hiding. "Only the best for you, Mr. W." Connie had always served his dinner on fine china. The cat crept out and began lapping, his little tongue flicking in and out a mile a minute. Poor thing.

Well, that settled it. Connie could not have set that blaze herself—not when her beloved cat might be harmed. Glory knew that Tyler thought Connie and Max had engineered the explosions to destroy evidence and create a diversion while they made their escape. But Glory didn't embrace that theory. She remembered how much Connie had treasured her antiques, many of them purchased from Glory Days. Her house was exquisitely decorated, each piece lovingly polished. She wouldn't have torched own home. Nor would she have left her journal and other evidence that incriminated her and Max for the police to find.

Of course, now Glory realized that she'd never really known her "friend." The suspicions she'd begun to have when she'd logged onto Ron's computer were now confirmed. Her best friends had killed her husband and Slade and run a drug ring.

Glory was beginning to question her own instincts. If she was wrong about their friendship, could she also have been wrong about Connie's love for antiques and for Mr. Whiskers? *No, surely not!* Maybe greed had driven Connie into drug dealing, but she did love beautiful things and appreciate fine furniture. And without question, Connie loved her cat. Glory had often wondered how her friend could afford so many valuable antiques. Now she knew.

But if Connie and Max didn't blow up their house, who did? And where were they now? Had they discovered they were in danger and run for the hills? Or had they been murdered too? Perhaps by a competitor in the drug trade. Glory sat at her desk in the back of the shop and tried to concentrate on paying her bills, but her mind kept returning to these questions and others she could not answer.

And who killed Tom Rankin and Elise Ashford? The police didn't think Connie and Max had done it. So who did? They'd mentioned a suspect named Flopsy. Really? *Flopsy*? Why would a killer have the name of an adorable rabbit?

Glory considered other possibilities. Maybe Scott Ashford was the killer. He certainly had been furious about his missing deed. His ex-wife Elise must have taken it and Tom, or someone impersonating him, had somehow obtained it and sent it to Glory. Were Elise and Tom working together? Would that make Scott angry enough to kill them both?

Then there was Lilly. Glory didn't want to believe that another person she liked and trusted had betrayed her. But Lilly had been at the fair and her story about finding the envelope on the counter was not completely convincing. Could *she* be Flopsy?

Glory's phone pinged. She picked it up and saw Joey's face on the screen. It was a video message. Glory she gasped in horror. Her son had been badly beaten, his cheek bruised, his eye black and swollen. There was a cut over his eye and blood trickled down his cheek. Joey moaned, "Don't you dare hurt my mom—" His weak voice trailed off. The camera pulled back to show that Joe was tied to a chair by duct tape. The screen went blank.

"Oh, Joey, sweetheart, what happened? Where are you?"

But of course, Joey couldn't hear her. Some sick person had taped the video and sent it to Glory via text.

Glory screamed. "No!" She replayed the video, desperate for clues. Where was he? She had to get to Joey—her youngest, her baby.

The phone rang. "I warned you," a voice rasped on the other end of the line. "I said someone close to you would be hurt if you didn't give it to me."

"What do you want? I'll give you anything I can. Just let Joey go."

"You know what you have to do."

"Tell me."

"Get it. Bring it to the store."

"The bear? Is that what you want? I don't have it."

"Get it. Bring it to your shop."

"And leave it here?"

"No. I want to see that you haven't tricked me. Be at the store with the bear at nine o'clock tonight. And another thing. If you tell the cops, your boy, Tyler, will be the first one I shoot. Then Joe. Two down." The creepy, hoarse voice laughed, sending shivers up and down Glory's spine.

Then whoever it was hung up.

Glory was terrified. If this sinister guy wanted her to bring the bear, not just leave it, he must mean to kill her. And it was very unlikely he was going to let Joe go, no matter what she did. Glory took a deep cleansing breath. Now in crisis mode, she focused on what must be done.

Painful as it was to watch, she played the video of Joe over and over, looking for clues in the background that would reveal where he was. He was tied by duct tape to a rustic, twisted-twig chair, and behind him was a stone fireplace. Where had she had seen that room before? Then she recognized it! Joey was in the Disney-type cottage on Scott Ashford's property, the one that she and Connie had thought was so magical. Could Scott be the man with the disguised voice? Or had someone else discovered this place? Maybe Max. Connie could have shown him where it was.

In any case, Glory knew what she had to do. She texted Tyler, "Call me. It's urgent."

In a minute, she heard Tyler's voice, a slight edge of impatience to it. "Mom, what is it? I'm at work."

"Watch this video." She forwarded it.

"Oh lord."

"Tyler, I know where Joey's being held. You have to go there. Bring back-up and be very careful."

"How did you find out where he is? Did the kidnapper tell you?"

"I don't have time to explain. Just do what I say."

"I need more information."

"Tyler, this is your mother speaking. Do it."

"Mom, I'm not six years old."

"Your brother's life is in danger. We don't have time to argue. Listen carefully. Joe's in a cottage with a peaked roof and shutters on Scott Ashford's land in Queens County. Go north on Highway Seven, then two miles west on Highway Four. Drive a half a mile farther on a one-lane country road that turns into Ashford's driveway. Wear your bullet-proof vest." Glory was glad that she had been so nervous about going out to the property with Scott Ashford that she had memorized the route.

"Okay. I wish I had more information, but I'll do it. I have to admit that video is very convincing…and scary. Poor Joe. Where are you, Mom?"

"In the shop."

"You're not planning on going out to the cottage yourself are you?"

He knew her all too well. If Glory didn't have to get the bear, she'd already be rushing to Joey's side like an enraged tigress. "Of course not," she assured him. "This is a job for the police. A dangerous job."

"Right. Did you get a call? A request for ransom or anything of that nature?" Tyler was back in cop mode now.

Glory crossed her fingers. "No." She kept her answer short, well aware that if she elaborated, Tyler would know she was lying.

"If you do, call me right away. Don't do anything the kidnapper asks you to do."

Glory took a deep breath.

"Did you hear me, Mom? Just stay where you are, or better yet, go home. Lock all the doors."

"Good idea. I'll go right home." Glory was relieved not to have to tell another lie. She'd go home to get Ron's gun and the keys to the police station. She had to get the bear.

Back home, Glory heard Cam cooking in the kitchen. She guessed that Chance was either upstairs or out. She moved carefully through the living room and into the den. She went to the safe where Ron kept his Glock, his bullet-proof vest, and the keys to the station. His vest was too big on her but it was better than nothing. This would be hazardous duty. She grabbed one of Ron's sweatshirts and pulled it on over the vest. Then she tiptoed out the front door before Cam or anyone else could spot her.

A few minutes later, Glory pulled up in front of the police station and used Ron's key to get inside. By now, the lights were out and the station looked completely deserted. Good. She hoped all the officers were on their way to rescue Joe. The video would certainly have convinced Ned Walker that Joe was truly in danger and he'd have mobilized his officers.

Suddenly, she heard a voice. "Stop where you are. I've got you in my sights."

Glory pressed her back against the wall. Then she realized the voice was drifting down from the second floor where the night watchman had his office. It was just the TV. Glory sighed in relief. Ron had told her that old Enoch was hard of hearing and kept his programs blasting. All the better. The TV soundtrack would mask the noise of Glory's own activities.

The evidence room was locked and Glory didn't have the key but Ron had told her how to get inside. She remembered him mentioning years ago that this loophole needed to be fixed but she suspected that no one had never gotten around to it.

She took a ladder out of the supply closet and leaned it against the outside wall of the evidence room, then climbed until she was close to the top rung. She reached up and pushed on a ceiling panel, knocking it to the ground. She waited a moment in silence, hoping Enoch hadn't heard the clatter. After a few seconds, she poked her head inside the ceiling and saw that the opening at the top of the evidence room wall was still there. The space was large enough to allow her to get in. Now Glory was glad that the new chief had been lax in getting this entry point fixed. Or was there more to it? Was it possible that Ned had left it this way on purpose? Glory realized that she didn't trust anyone but her own family anymore.

Now for the hard part. Thank goodness she'd been doing pushups and squats every day down at the Y. She was ready for the challenge. *Maybe*. Through the opening in front of her she could see into the room where shelves holding evidence reached to the ceiling on all sides. Glory crawled onto the top of the ladder, teetering precariously, then pulled herself through the opening in the ceiling. She stretched out her arms and grabbed at the topmost shelf. Then she gathered all her strength and pulled her body the rest of the way through the opening, kicking the ladder over in the process. There was no time to waste hoping Enoch hadn't heard that one. She lowered herself down into the evidence room, stepping carefully from shelf to shelf.

Once she touched down on the floor, she caught her breath and scanned the shelves. There on the bottom, she found her bear, its pink stuffing poking out from the incision in its belly. Apparently the mysterious caller hadn't known the money had been found and removed. Cash was always stored in the safe in the evidence room. Glory didn't know the combination so she would have to figure out a way to disguise the fact that the money was gone.

The evidence room wasn't locked from the inside so Glory simply opened the door and walked out. From upstairs, she heard a TV voice blaring, "I thought you had my back. Fine partner you turned out to be." Glory left the building with the bear tucked under her arm.

After a quick stop at a newsstand to buy a paper, Glory drove back to her shop. She let herself in the back door, went down to the basement that the three shops shared, and found the storage area for the toy store. She knew the play money was kept near the cardboard kiddie grocery store along with the plastic fruits and vegetables and mini boxes of cereal and cookies. Glory scooped a thick stack of dollars from the little toy cash register. Then she went upstairs to the office in back of her shop.

Something soft slithered around her ankles and Glory almost screamed, then realized what it was and turned on the light. Mr. Whiskers meowed a couple of times. The poor thing was hungry! Glory reached into her purse and found a half-eaten energy bar.

"Sorry, Mr. Whiskers. This is all I've got." She crumbled it into a faux Ming saucer and set it on the floor. The cat dug in.

There wasn't much time before the kidnapper would arrive. Glory hastily shredded some newspaper pages, stuffed them into the bear, placed the toy dollars on top, then added some fives and tens from her wallet. This would have to do. Maybe he wouldn't look too closely.

As she tried to sew up the bear, Glory's fingers trembled. Her fear for her two sons made it hard to concentrate on the task at hand. Had Tyler and Ned and the other officers managed to rescue Joe? What was happening? Glory texted Tyler. *"Is Joe okay? Are you okay? What's up?"* There was no answer. The suspense was unbearable.

After Glory finally finished her sewing, the bear didn't look bad at all. It was almost showtime—ten minutes to nine o'clock. Glory didn't turn on the lights in the front of the store. She wanted to plan a special welcome for the man who had beaten her youngest son and who most likely intended to kill her as well. Years ago, she and Slade had practiced shooting together. Back then, he had said she was a natural. Then Ron, in his turn, had encouraged her to keep up her skills at the firing range. He used to call her Dead Eye Glory. Of course, Ron had chuckled when he'd said it, but Glory took heart as she remembered that she was a competent shot. And she intended to have the advantage of surprise on her side. The criminal would expect her to be waiting meekly in the corner, not pointing a Glock directly at his chest for maximum chance of injury.

Glory tucked the bear into the antique pram and centered it in the middle of the store. Then she focused a lamp on it like a spotlight, directing attention. Where to station herself? She didn't want to be seen right away.

Then it came to her. She went over to the mannequin and took off its vintage red, white and blue dress. She hastily slipped it on. It wouldn't fasten in back because of her bullet-proof vest, but that didn't matter. She put on the white, wide-brimmed hat and moved into the shadows. Her heart was pounding. Glory had never shot anyone, and she didn't want to start now. Best case scenario, the sinister guy would grab the bear and when he saw she had a gun, run out the door. She hoped he'd be wearing a mask so she wouldn't be able to identify him later. If not, he would have to kill her. Glory put her finger on the trigger and let out a shallow breath.

The bell that announced visitors tinkled and the door flew open. Gunfire rang out, spraying bullets around the store.

"You!" Glory cried as she stepped out of the shadows, raised the Glock, and fired.

Chapter 19
by Elizabeth Jukes

Her shot found its mark in a kneecap. The intruder's gun clattered to the floor and there was a shriek of pain.

"Next time, don't mess with a mother," Glory muttered through gritted teeth.

Howling and cursing spewed from the writhing figure on the floor. Glory felt softness swirling around her ankle. Mr. Whiskers was surveying the scene. Singed fur and whiskerless face notwithstanding, he stepped serenely over to the moaner and promptly sat on her chest.

"He seems comfy there," said Glory, moving to pick up the fallen gun. Her Glock stayed steadily trained on the kidnapper. "Don't move. You've still got another kneecap I could shoot for."

"Glory…"

Glory snatched up the gun. "Glory? Are you praying? If not, you'd better. And it's *Mrs. Lockhart* to you." Glory set the kidnapper's gun beside the teddy in the pram and twitched out a blanket. "Here," she said, holding it out. "Wrap it around your knee. I'm going to make some calls and then we'll talk."

Glory wasn't sure just how much she'd learn since the shattered kneecap was probably excruciating, but she was determined to try. With her left hand, she fetched her cell phone out of the dress' pocket and speed dialed Cameron.

"Mom! Where are you?"

"At the shop. Don't ask questions just follow my instructions. Get an ambulance sent here for a shooting victim. Not life threatening. Not me—don't worry. Call Tyler and tell him Joey's kidnapper and Tom Rankin's murderer has been captured and to send the FBI agents. Then come to the shop."

"Wow, okay."

Glory pocketed her phone.

"So," she began, eyeing a black widow spider tattoo on the woman's bare arm. "Mala—or Flopsy? Which do you prefer?"

No answer, just a glare as the young woman pushed Mr. Whiskers off her chest and dragged herself backwards to a wall, leaning against it and panting.

"Let me do you a favor. I'll spin a story for you which will help keep your mind off the pain. Let's start with recent events. There was once a down-home couple named Connie and Max who liked to, hmm, trade in spices—nutmeg which would soon be myristicin, to be precise. They managed to hoodwink everyone in their town and had created a robust business for themselves. Now, there was another woman who also traded in spices—but she liked carnivals. She traveled in rarefied circles—I even recall seeing her once at a party talking to some high government officials who probably had no idea of her other 'job.' One day in her carnival traveling she met up with the nice couple and suggested they do business together. But somehow they didn't play fair so she blew up their house. All in a day's work."

Glory removed the wide-brimmed hat, tossing it into the pram which now held a very odd assortment of things.

"I'm assuming you believed they were inside when you struck the match?"

Still no answer.

"By the way. Teddy there has no money in him."

This got a response. "What? You wouldn't dare!"

"I wouldn't dare what? Come without the money? You underestimated me, and apparently you aren't familiar with the workings of the police. All evidentiary money is kept in a safe."

"Con and Max should never've set you up with Tom. Insanely stupid blunder. Bringing the former chief's wife into it and her son on the force? Idiots."

"Hmm, now that you put it that way that was rather foolish of them."

Mr. Whiskers had taken up a sphinx-like position on the floor between the two women. Mala/Flopsy sneezed. She groaned as the eruption caused a jolt of pain to the injured knee.

"Why did you kill Elise Ashford? You might as well talk—it's a good distraction. The ambulance will still be a few minutes."

Another glare. "I needed the deed. She was going to sell the property. I needed the place kept in the family."

"You're an Ashford?"

"Scott is my uncle." Mala caught her breath in pain.

"But why did Tom have it?"

"He didn't. I was just muddying the waters by making you the messenger and signing his name."

"Water. You wanted access to the property because of the river. Easier to transport your drugs."

"It being my uncle's land meant he wouldn't ever question why I might want to *enjoy* it."

"How did you get my son to that cottage?" Glory asked angrily.

"Simple. I left him a note on your back door saying you needed him there. Once there, a knock over the head made it easy to tie him up. I'm good at copying handwriting styles."

Glory felt like using the gun again.

"What is Scott Ashford's role in all this?"

"Scott!" exclaimed Mala scornfully. "Nothing."

Glory pondered. Mala closed her eyes and clenched her jaw.

"How did you deliver the note about the deed to my store?" Her questioning was all over the map, but she didn't care. She wanted all the loose ends tied up in her mind.

"Through the toy store's basement door and up into your store. You people really should lock your doors."

"How did you kill Tom?"

"I enjoyed a ride on the Ferris wheel."

"But you were the ticket taker."

"It's my carnival. I can hand off jobs as I like."

Carnival. It suddenly came to Glory. *I must lie down where all the ladders start in the foul rag and bone shop of the heart.* The last line in William Butler Yeats' poem, "The Circus Animals Desertion." Slade *had* been trying to give her a message. It was a poem they had studied in school. She had hated it and so had quickly forgotten it, but with Connie standing right there with them that day at Nutmeg's, it was the best Slade could do to bring a carnival to her mind. He knew she'd eventually remember!

"But why the rifle scope?"

"Oh, that was plan A. Someone else was to kill Tom—a loyalty test." Mala gave a little shrug. "He balked. When the carriage behind you was still empty, I decided to take it and ditched the scope."

"Who balked?"

No answer—just a smug smile.

The sirens that Glory had been hearing in the distance were quickly becoming louder and through the door she could see a swirl of red light announcing the imminent arrival of the ambulance.

"Was it your idea to kill my husband?"

Mala grinned maliciously. "Oh no. That was all Max and Con."

It didn't take the paramedics long to transfer Mala to a stretcher. Just as she was being carried out the door, Cameron arrived and Glory could hear another siren in the wake of the first.

"I believe that's the FBI," she said to the paramedics. "Could you wait just a moment for them to read this woman her rights and arrest her? She's killed, kidnapped, and is a drug runner among other things."

They all turned toward the car as it swung around the corner. Two doors flew open and agents Steele and Sherman jumped out.

"This is Mala DeTritus," said Glory, indicating the pale woman on the stretcher. "Also known as Flopsy— at least to the Robertsons."

"Yes, Ms. DeTritus has been on our radar for a few years now. Originally from New Jersey but expanding her territory," said Agent Sherman.

"Spreading her web as it were," said Glory, nodding at the tattoo on Mala's arm. Both agents smiled grimly. "Ms. DeTritus has confessed to the murder of Tom Rankin and Elise Ashford as well as the explosion at the Robertsons', but I'm sure there are plenty of other things she could tell you."

Suddenly, it was as though the events of the evening caught up with Glory, and she felt lightheaded and overcome with exhaustion. She realized she was still gripping the Glock and looked around blankly unsure what to do with it.

"Here, Mom," said Cameron gently, holding his hand out. "Give it to me." He led her to a Chippendale dining room chair into which she slumped gratefully.

She smiled up at her son. "I bet I look just how I wanted the mannequin in the window to look—minus this bulky vest, of course."

Cameron squeezed her hand.

Through the open shop door Glory could hear that the agents were doing their job. Then the ambulance attendants continued with theirs. She knew that at the hospital Mala would be guarded around the clock. That was a relief. But…

Another official vehicle pulled up in front of the store, interrupting her thought process. She was following some thread that she couldn't quite grasp. She looked at the car and saw Tyler and Ned and— glory be!—Joey, bloodied but unbowed.

There were moments as a parent when one needed to sob hysterically with relief and joy. This was one of those moments, but Glory knew that her emotional release would have to wait. Instead she inhaled deeply, stood up, and walked over to meet her sons, holding out a hand to each. "I'm so proud of both of you, and your dad would be, too."

Glory Days was ribboned off as a crime scene. Officers turned on all the lights and brought in extra lights on stands. They discovered where Mala's bullets had slammed into the wall opposite the door. They retrieved her gun from the pram. Teddy was going for a ride again in a cruiser back to the station. If only he could talk, he would have made an excellent witness. Ned Walker took down Glory's statement. Nobody said anything about a civilian taking the law into her own hands. It would have to be said eventually but they were treating her with kid gloves for the moment. She herself attended to Joey, washing his cuts and applying witch hazel to his bruises. Glory would remember all of this through a haze. There was, of course, the plummet from the adrenaline rush that comes when danger is faced, but even more than that was the bruising to her soul. Her friends, those she thought were dear friends, had planned and implemented her husband's murder.

The next morning Glory woke up to sunshine and birdsong. She lay still with her eyes closed, breathing deeply and listening to the happy chorus. It occurred to her that all the wickedness that people perpetuate couldn't stop the sun from rising or the birds from singing. Somehow that realization was a gift. It helped to lift the weight of last night's terror and darkness and anger and grief. There was a tap on her door and it slowly swung open.

"Hey," said Lilly coming in carrying a tray. Glory could smell coffee and spied the round rise of fresh croissants. "When I saw the yellow police tape at the store I figured we wouldn't be open today." She smiled wryly.

Glory actually laughed. "Very astute of you." She looked at her bedside clock. "Nine thirty! It can't be!"

Glory pulled herself upright and Lilly nestled the tray onto the bed. They each reached for a mug of coffee, regarding one other over the rims.

"Lilly, I—" Glory began.

But Lilly held up a hand. "There's nothing to say."

Glory teared up. "Thank you."

"Chief Walker was at the store when I went in so I also come bearing the message that he would like to see you at the station sometime today."

"Yes, I bet he would."

"Hey, Mom," said Joey, shambling into her room and flopping on the bed. "Too bad school's done. I could've shown off my battle scars." He eyed the tray. "Do you want both of those croissants?"

She smiled tenderly at him. Oh, the rebounding exuberance of youth.

"Go away, Joey. One of those is mine," retorted Lilly.

He sighed dramatically and heaved himself off the bed.

Chance poked his head around the door. "You ready, Joe? Hey, Mom. I'm taking him out for breakfast. How are you?"

"I'm fine."

"Good." He fumbled with his keys. "You're amazing," he said with a quiet grin.

Joey glanced back as he went out the door. "Yeah. Thanks, Mom."

The two women looked at each other.

Glory chuckled. "It almost makes all this other stuff worthwhile."

"This is good timing," said Chief Walker when Glory presented herself at the police station shortly after one that afternoon. "Agents Sherman and Steele are here. How are you?"

"Actually, I'm doing quite well."

"Very glad to hear it. Now. On to police business. What you did was dangerous, *and* you withheld information pertinent to a case, *and* you removed evidence without permission. Nobody is above the law, Glory. The law is what keeps us safe. I've talked Sherman and Steele into letting me deal with you rather than the FBI. So, here's what's going to happen. I'm going to charge you and write you up and fine you. The fine will be ten dollars, which can be settled out of court. Then I'll file it." He glanced towards a corner waste basket.

"Thank you, Ned, uh, Chief Walker."

"Have a seat please, Mrs. Lockhart. We'll take care of these charges and then meet with the federal agents. They've offered to let you know a few details."

In the ten minutes it took for Sherman and Steele to finish their lunches, Glory was charged, fined, and released. When she and the chief entered the conference room, he nodded to the agents who nodded back. Glory's criminal career was over and done with.

Agent Steele balled up the plastic wrap from his sandwich and lobbed it into a corner wastebasket. "Before her surgery this morning," he began, "Ms. DeTritus filled in some blanks for us. Going back to the night of Tom Rankin's murder, she confirmed that Slade was there. He was wearing a clown costume. It was likely Slade that Tom was looking at from the Ferris wheel. DeTritus had ordered him to kill Tom. He couldn't and-or wouldn't do it."

"Yes, she said she was testing someone's loyalty, but she wouldn't tell me who," said Glory.

"We think it was then that his cover was blown," said Sherman.

Glory and Ned nodded.

"So then, as you know, she took the matter into her own hands," continued Steele. "The Nutmeg, LLC, was a front, of course. When DeTritus moved into the area a few years ago she saw Slade's restaurant and thought the name would be amusing to use as an empty corporation to cover her business. It allowed her to provide staff for carnivals and if anything went wrong in any of the ensuing drug deals, there was no tracing them. All the carnival staff are users courtesy of her, of course, so no questions were asked."

"What about the quarter million dollars in the bear?" Glory asked.

"That was the money DeTritus was going to pay Slade to kill Tom," said Sherman. "It was a fluke that the bear ended up in Tom's hands. Most people at a carnival shooting gallery aren't going to do so well as to be able to choose whatever prize they want. DeTritus figured no one would even think about the bear."

"So somehow she had begun to suspect Slade," said Glory. "What a muddle. Two brothers doing the same job but one thinks the other is the bad guy."

"Right," said Sherman abruptly. He rose from his seat and held out his hand to shake Glory's. "I think that wraps up what we have so far. You've done us a service without question, but in the future, do leave this work to us."

Steele rose and shook Glory's hand as well, and Chief Walker escorted her to the station door.

"We'll try and have the store ready for business in a day or two. Life will soon be back to normal," he assured her.

On the station steps she took a deep breath. *Normal.* At the moment she wasn't sure what normal was. She slowly descended the steps and out of the corner of her eye, she saw a uniformed officer. She scanned the block ahead of her. There was another. It was then that the thread of thought she hadn't been able to grasp last night pulled itself taut in her brain. Her son had said drug lords don't like loose ends. Connie and Max were still at large, and Glory would be considered a loose end.

Chapter 20
by Patricia Rockwell

Exhaustion forced Glory to sleep, but it was a fitful one, and she now found herself wide awake in the middle of the night feeling nervous and anxious. As she glanced over to her nightstand, the sight of her purse kindled a thought and she reached for the bag and scrounged around deep inside until she extracted the envelope with the lavender letter from Ron that she'd found hidden in the Shakespeare tome in her storage room.

Setting her purse on the floor beside the bed, she clutched the envelope to her heart. She gently caressed the paper, knowing that the last person to touch it was her husband. She breathed in deeply, almost as if she could smell his scent from the paper. Of course, this was impossible; the letter had been stuck between pages of an old book for months. Even so, Glory pressed against the envelope as if it were Ron's cheek.

"Oh, Ron," she said aloud. "Why didn't you just tell me all of this? Maybe . . ."

But Glory was too practical to dwell on "could-have-beens" for long, and soon she had opened the envelope, turned on her bedside lamp, and was diligently rereading the section she'd already read in the storage room, and then continuing on with the remaining section that she had not yet been able to look at.

In the remainder of the letter, Ron went on to detail for Glory what he knew about the drug ring that had spread its tentacles through their small community.

Although Glory realized that he hadn't yet tumbled to Connie and Max's involvement, he did warn Glory that the conspiracy was pervasive and probably involved well-placed individuals who were above reproach.

"Oh, Ron," whispered Glory, "if you only knew. . ." Had her husband suspected their friends Connie and Max?

The letter did mention that Ron had discovered the drug ring's use of a widespread network of tunnels in the area for transporting their illegal goods. Ron had evidently found some of these tunnels himself and was working on tracking down more of them. Of course, he had to go carefully because if he ran into any of the crooks while exploring the tunnels, he would have little defense.

Glory was surprised that Ron noted in his letter that he had not informed Ned of his findings, but he listed for her the names, addresses, and dates of various individuals in the area he'd discovered who were involved in the drug ring. Glory was surprised to see the names of a few well-known and respected businessmen in Rainbow's End. She resolved to get Ron's letter to Ned first thing in the morning and chided herself for not showing it to him earlier in the day.

As she glanced at her nightstand alarm clock, she saw that it was now three a.m. She'd finished reading the entire letter but doubted she could return to sleep. Glancing up at her window, she heard a footstep in the hallway. She assumed it was Joey or Chance making a middle of the night bathroom break. However, the footstep came closer to her door and she heard the doorknob slowly start to turn.

Thinking it unlikely that either of her sons would be checking on her in the middle of the night, she quickly bent over the side of her bed and reached underneath where she had placed Ron's Glock instead of returning it to his safe after her recent adventure. Grabbing the gun, she quickly moved from the near side of her bed and positioned herself behind the door, gun poised.

One more turn of the knob and the door inched open. Slowly a woman moved into the room. She was visible in a slight glow from the hallway nightlight. Just like Glory, she too was holding a gun.

"Come in, Connie," said Glory, standing behind her, pointing the Glock at her friend. Connie said nothing but took a few steps inside the bedroom then gently turned and faced her accuser. Her eyes never left Glory.

"How'd you get by Ned's deputies?" said Glory.

"Tunnels," said Connie with a shrug. "There's one that comes out behind the washer in your basement. I just had to cut through some plasterboard. Ron had no idea." She smiled.

Hearing her supposed friend say her husband's name made Glory itch to pull the trigger of the Glock.

"Don't even mention. . . .Where's Max?"

"Oh, he's too big to fit through the tunnel into your basement—so this job is all mine. He's waiting in the tunnels that lead into a drainage ditch near the entrance to your farm." She smiled again. "Now, Glory, we both know you couldn't shoot that thing . . . at least, you couldn't shoot it at a person . . . especially me—your best friend." She smiled again.

"You don't think so? You can ask your friend, Mala. I took out her kneecap this afternoon."

Connie was silent.

"How did this happen? How did you get this way, Connie?" Glory felt the emotion in her throat.

"I like nice things."

"You killed my husband!" cried Glory.

Connie shrugged. "He discovered our tunnels. It wouldn't have been long and he would have realized that they extended under his own home . . . Glory, I don't have time for this reverie. It would have been so much easier if you'd been asleep . . . Now we're going to have to have some sort of shoot out." She bit her lip and seemed to be thinking . . . or planning as she glanced around the room out of the corner of her eye. She inched closer to Glory, lifting her gun upward with a menacing shove. Glory inched backwards toward the bed, almost stumbling but catching herself with her free hand. Still, she steadily maintained the Glock's position aimed at Connie.

"Yes," said Connie, coming closer to Glory. "Let's get you back onto your bed." She gestured with her gun for Glory to get on the bed.

"No!" replied Glory suddenly, standing upright and waving the Glock at Connie. "*You* back up!"

Startled, Connie, almost despite herself, took a step backwards and lost her balance, toppling over an ottoman behind her. As she fell, her gun clattered to the floor and slid under Glory's lounge chair. Connie quickly rolled over to her knees and tried to reach under the chair, but Glory was too quick. She grabbed Connie by the back of her pants and pulled hard with her free hand. Connie struggled to get loose, still reaching under the chair for her gun. Realizing that she was losing ground, Glory dropped the Glock so she could grab Connie's pants with both hands, which she did, pulling with all her might. Glory's efforts caused Connie's body to slide on the slick wooden floor away from the chair and towards the center of the bedroom where Glory then jumped on top of her friend with a loud yelp.

Within a few seconds, Joey and Chance arrived from their bedrooms and pulled the women apart. Cam hurried up from the guest room on the main floor.

"Where did she come from?" cried Joey.

"How did she get in?" said Chance. "Where were the deputies?"

"The washing machine," replied Glory, breathless.

"*What?*" Even in their confusion, Glory's sons held Connie tightly while she ran downstairs and called out the front door to the deputies who both came inside quickly and hustled up the stairs into Glory's bedroom.

"How'd she get past us?" yelled one.

"Didn't see her!" said the other. "Where'd she come from?"

"Behind the washing machine," Glory again replied. "Just go look and you'll see!" As all five men stared at Glory, she took a deep breath, now totally winded from her struggle and from running up and down the stairs. "They built tunnels—the drug ring. One lets out right behind our washer in our basement. Max is still down there; she said he's waiting for her. The tunnel is supposed to come out near the drainage ditch by our property entrance. I'd start there." At that, Glory collapsed onto the bed and the two deputies gave each other quick mystified glances and then hightailed it back out of the bedroom, one calling the crime in on his walkie-talkie as he ran. Glory could hear them leave through the front door, heading towards the property's main entrance.

Joey and Chance lifted Connie from the floor and pulled her out of Glory's bedroom. Cameron followed them out, calling back over his shoulder, "You okay, Mom, if we . . .?"

"Yes, go . . ."

The three men dragged Connie down the stairs to the sound of the Sheriff's siren in the distance.

As she slowly gathered her breath, Glory took the envelope with the purple pages and tucked it back into her purse for safekeeping. There would be plenty of time to read it again—and again.

Several years later, long after Connie and Max Robertson had been tried, sentenced, and incarcerated for their crimes—particularly, Connie's murder of Ron Lockhart—long after Chief Walker along with his deputies and the FBI had located, explored, and then closed all of the drug-running tunnels in the area around Rainbow's End, long after the drug cartel that operated in the vicinity with such ease had either been jailed or had moved on due to local and federal pressure—long after this—the carnival came back to Rainbow's End. This time it was run by a different company.

At the county fairgrounds, Glory and her new beau were wandering around the carnival, sipping colas.

"Want to ride the Ferris wheel?" her boyfriend asked.

"Sure you want to risk it?" she replied.

"You mean because of your checkered history with doing in your dates on these things?" the man asked with a twinkle in his eye.

"That, and maybe what might happen if we find ourselves alone together at the top?" Glory smiled.

He took a good look at the lovely widow. "Think I'll chance it."

The couple climbed into the ride's small compartment. The wheel turned and soon they found themselves stopping at the top, overlooking the entire fairgrounds. And, as before, there *was* an explosion—but not the type involving firearms. Just one smoldering kiss.

When the wheel returned Glory and her beau to the ground, both were alive—very much alive. And the wheel of death was just a distant memory.

THE END

ABOUT THE AUTHORS

 **Bart J. Gilbertson** is the author of the Pookotz Sisters Bed and Breakfast mystery series. Although he was born in Wisconsin, he spent most of his youth and later years in the rocky mountain state of Idaho. Bart has been all over the northwest and it is his love for the lush green state of Oregon that inspired the setting for Pleasant Lake and its inhabitants. *Deathbed & Breakfast* is his first novel. He attended ITT Tech and received an Associate in Applied Science Degree for Computer Networking Systems and graduated with honors. Bart has worn many hats over his lifetime career, but the one he is most proud of is that of being a writer. He currently resides in O'Neill, NE. He has two children.

 **Annie Irvin** has enjoyed a nomadic life and after inheriting her grandfather's large collection of books still managed to always find room in the U-Haul for every last page even if it meant leaving behind the kitchen table. Eventually, Annie ended up where she began—a small town in Iowa where gossip is king and scandal has ruined more than one good woman, although no one has yet resorted to murder.

 **Rae Sanders** once consulted an honest-to-goodness fortune teller who predicted she'd be married three times and wouldn't find true happiness until she lived near the water. Not a swimmer, Rae scoffed at the idea. However, she is now happily married to

husband number three and lives in Minnesota, Land of 10,000 Lakes. When she isn't writing, she's fishing for supper. Annie and Rae are sisters who became addicted to reading cozy mysteries while in their teens. Today they enjoy every minute spent creating the characters that live, love, and, alas, die in Bittersweet Hollow. Their books include *Final Sale* and *Down a Deadly River*.

Jennifer Vido is best known for her nationally syndicated *Jen's Jewels* author interview column. A savvy book blogger for www.MomTrends.com, she dishes the scoop on the latest happenings in the publishing business. As a national spokesperson for the Arthritis Foundation, she has been featured by *Lifetime Television, Redbook, Health Monitor, The New York Times, The Baltimore Sun, Healthguru.com,* and *Arthritis Today*. Her first novel *Par for the Course* was published in 2010. Currently, she lives in the Baltimore area with her husband and two sons. Visit her website at www.jennifervido.com and follow her on Twitter @JenniferVido. For Cozy Cat Press she writes the Piper O'Donnell Social Lite mysteries which include *Country Clubbed* and *Murder by the Minutes*.

Laura Shea is a professor of English at Iona College. She is the author of *A Moon for the Misbegotten on the American Stage*, and her essays and reviews have appeared in *The Eugene O'Neill Review, Theatre Journal, Theatre Annual, The Comparatist,* and *American Theater Web*. She has also worked in different professional capacities in theaters in Boston and New York. In addition to *Murder at the People's Theater* for Cozy Cat Press, she is also the author of *A Dying Fall*, a mystery novel set in academe. She lives in New York.

 **Emma Pivato** and her husband, Joe, have raised three children—the youngest, Alexis, having multiple challenges. Their efforts to organize the best possible life for her have provided some of the background context for the Claire Burke mystery series. The society that the Pivatos have formed to support Alexis in her adult years is described at http://www.homewithinahome.com/Main.html. Emma's other cozy mysteries are entitled *Blind Sight Solution, Deadly Care, The Crooked Knife, Roscoe's Revenge, Jessie Knows,* and *Murder on Highway 2*.

 **Joyce Oroz** is not only passionate about her writing, painting and large family, she loves being involved in her community. Aromas, California is a very small town, perfect for working with friends and neighbors. Oroz' most recent endeavor was helping children paint their zucchinis—as in squash, for the zucchini races at the Harvest Festival. She also has a real soft spot for the annual county fair and loves to bring that small-town flavor into her stories. Her Josephine Stuart mysteries include *Cuckoo Clock Caper, Hill Street Clues, Pushing Up Daisy, Roller Rubout, Scent of a $windle,* and *Who Killed Mary Christmas?*

 **Christian Belz** has been a practicing architect in Metro Detroit for 28 years, with experience in retail, educational, and industrial projects. He is Vice President of Detroit Working Writers. He won the Grand Prize in Aquarius Press's 2011 Bright Harvest Prize for his short story *Chambers*. Christian's fiction has appeared in *Writers' Journal, The Story Teller Magazine*, and Wicked East Press's anthology: *Short Sips, Coffee House Flash Fiction Collection 2*. His poetry has been published in *WestWard Quarterly* and *Yes, Poetry*. Christian is one of the co-authors of *The 28-Day Thought Diet*. His blog *Real life, love and growth* can be found at ChristianBelz.org. *The Accused Architect* and *Civic Center Corpse* are the two Ken Knoll Architectural mysteries he wrote for Cozy Cat Press.. Look for Christian's author page on Goodreads.

 **Pam 'T'Gracie' Reese** is an assistant professor of communication sciences and disorders at Indiana University-Purdue University Fort Wayne (IPFW). Her main character Nina Bannister was created while T'Gracie was a doctoral student at the University of Louisiana-Lafayette. She has happy memories of exploring Acadiana, dancing the Cajun waltz, catching beads at Mardi Gras and listening to French on the radio. (Geaux Cajuns!) Still, she also loves her new life in Ft. Wayne and enjoys getting to know northern Indiana. (Go Mastodons!). **Joe Reese** is a writer and teacher. He's only partially responsible for the Nina Bannister mysteries (co-written with his wife, T'Gracie)—*Sea*

Change, Set Change, Frame Change, Oil Change, Game Change, Bed Change, Sex Change, Mind Change, and Time Change published by Cozy Cat. However, he has to take full blame for *Kate Dee and Katie Haw: Letters from a Texas Farm Girl* and the play *Lunacy: A Play for Our Times*. He and his wife have three children: Kate, Matthew, and Sam. The two of them now live in Fort Wayne, Indiana, where each teaches at IPFW.

Trisha Durrant was raised in post-war Britain. After seeing an ad in the *London Times*, which said, 'Come to the sun-drenched desert of Arizona,' she immediately decided to emigrate. In her defense, it was raining at the time and she was an out of work actor who was tired of waiting on tables. Now four children, eight grand-children, many homes and too many cats to enumerate later, she lives in beautiful Asheville, North Carolina, with her remaining cat Monty, nicknamed "The Monster." *Almost Abducted* and *Body in the Barn* are the books in her new Kate and Doris Mystery series.

Owen Magruder is the *nom de plume* of a retired college professor. He has authored three professional books and a small volume of remembrances of the American Civil War. In addition, he and his wife have co-authored a brief biography of a little known abolitionist from upstate New York for the National Abolition Hall of Fame. From 1989 to 2005, the couple ran a small publishing house that specialized in original letters and journals from the American Civil War. Magruder's ancestral home is in the Scottish highlands, hence the Scottish link to his mystery novels. *The Feud at Glencoe and Other Adventures, Death at Beggar's Knob,* and *The Lost Pipers of Craig Dhuin* are three mysteries in his John and Mary Braemhor series for Cozy Cat. Owen Magruder resides in upstate New York.

 **David Selcer** authors the Buckeye Barrister mystery series, which includes *Deadly Audit, Dead But Still Ticking, Music, Muscles, and Murder,* and *Dreamcatcher Murders*. After graduating from Northwestern University, he attended Ohio State University Law School. He then had an exciting career practicing management labor law with a large national law firm for 35 years. Today, he lives with his wife for half the year in Sarasota, Florida, where he writes mysteries, and in Columbus, Ohio, the other half, which he still considers his home. He has five children and is an avid OSU Buckeye fan. He also continues to make employment case decisions for federal agencies on a part time basis as a Federal Agency Decision Writer.

 **Zaida Alfaro**'s novel for Cozy Cat is *The Last Note*. The main backdrop for the book is Miami, Florida, which is beloved and well-known to Zaida. She was born and raised in Miami, and like the novel's main character, Vy, is a singer/songwriter, as well as the lead singer to a self-proclaimed cover band. All things relating to music or literature are her passion. She keeps

a journal, and is constantly writing poems, stories. She has a fascination for black and white films, that have the element of mystery. Many years ago, Zaida became an avid reader of cozy mysteries. She was so inspired by the authors, that she then decided to take her musical experiences, and put it on paper. Zaida hopes that she was able to bring the love she has for Miami, the Cuban culture, her family, and music, to her readers.

Karen Shughart is the author of two non-fiction books, and has worked as an editor, publicist, photographer, journalist, and non-profit executive. *A Murder in the Museum: An Edmund DeCleryk Mystery* is her first work of fiction. Before moving to a small village on the shores of Lake Ontario in upstate New York, she and her husband resided in south central Pennsylvania, near Harrisburg, PA. For more information, you can visit her website at: www.karenshughart.com.

Lane Buckman is a former beauty queen from Phenix City, Alabama. Growing up, she wanted to be Miss America, a criminal lawyer, a super model, the President, a Bond girl, a brain surgeon, a journalist, a back-up singer for Duran Duran, and a college professor of Medieval Literature. In order to fulfill those dreams, she became a writer. She lives in Texas with her family, and enjoys every miserably hot second of it. Her mystery for Cozy Cat is *Tiara Trouble.*

Carmen Will is a freelance writer and editor whose novel, *A Practicum for Murder*, was a finalist in Poisoned Pen Press' 2013 Discover Mystery contest. Will, who earned a B.A. in Professional Communication with a specialization in writing and editing, lives in Sun Lakes, Arizona, with her husband Wayne. Her two Amanda Winters mysteries include *Doubly Departed* and *Deadly Degree.*

Leslie Matthews Stansfield is the author of *Mr. Tea and the Traveling Teacup* and *Mr. Tea and the Bobbin' Body,* of the Madeline's Teahouse series. She is the

author of a previous book about the town she lives in. She grew up in Delmar, New York, and credits her friends with developing her imagination. Leslie is a graduate of the University of Hartford and received her Masters' degree from the University of Phoenix in Educational Leadership. She is a math tutor in a public school as well as the Christian Education Director of her church. Leslie has four children and eight grandchildren and lives in Windsor Locks, Connecticut.

Julie Seedorf owns her own computer repair business, but her secret undercover job is writing. Her column "Something About Nothing" for a Minnesota

newspaper is about nothing, which is what we talk about most of the time, but with something underneath the conversation. She has been a wife, mother, grandmother, housewife, barmaid, salesperson, activity director, full time volunteer and more. Her motto is "If you dream it, you can do it." Her Fuchsia Minnesota, series is the first of her journey in her undercover career and includes *Granny Hooks a Crook, Granny Forks a Fugitive, Granny Pins a Pilferer, Granny Snows a Sneak* and *Granny Skewers a Scoundrel.* Having lived in small communities in Minnesota all her life, she knows the richness and uniqueness that only a small town can bring and with a little humor and imagination she transforms those experiences into her imaginary Fuchsia community.

Lorrie Holmgren is the author of *Murder on Madeline Island and Homicide in Hawaii.* Like her fictional heroine, Lorrie loves to travel and learn about the history, art and culture of other places. She grew up in Wilmette, Illinois, a suburb of Chicago, an ardent Cubs fan. Her lifelong love of travel began when she was eight years old and lived in Milan, Italy, with her Mom, Dad, and brother. It was an unforgettable year—skating in St. Moritz, visits to Sforza Castle, gondola rides, Easter in Florence, trips to art museums. She received a BA in English from Wells College in Aurora, New York, where she began to write short stories in a class taught by Mildred Walker, author of *Winter Wheat.*

Elizabeth Jukes has always enjoyed reading. Often, as a child, she would hold up a book to the light from the front porch lamp. All this, of course, when she was supposed to be asleep. Love of reading translated to love of writing. A

Journalism Diploma followed, as well as a Bachelor of Theology, and then, with life's twists, many years of no writing except for journaling. But a few years ago, the Dorothea Montgomery character appeared in her mind and the desire to flesh that all out in *Pin It on a Dead Man* was irresistible. Elizabeth lives in New Hamburg, Ontario, with her husband, Jon, and their two sons.

 **Patricia Rockwell** is the author of two mystery series. Her Pamela Barnes acoustic mysteries include *Sounds of Murder*, *FM For Murder*, *Voice Mail Murder*, *Stump Speech Murder*, and *Murder in the Round*. Her Essie Cobb senior sleuth mysteries include *Bingoed*, *Papoosed*, *Valentined*, *Ghosted*, and *Firecrackered*. She is the founder and publisher of Cozy Cat Press, which specializes in producing cozy (or gentle) mysteries. Dr. Rockwell is presently living in Aurora, Illinois, with her husband Milt, also a retired educator.

If you enjoyed *Wheel of Death*, we hope you will check out the books written by the authors of its individual chapters. You can find their works at: www.cozycatpress.com.

Also, please consider posting a review on your favorite retailer's website.